FAMILY GAME NIGHT

AND OTHER CATASTROPHES

AND OTHER CATASTROPHES

Mary E. Lambert

Scholastic Press / *New York*

Library of Congress Cataloging-in-Publication Data

Names: Lambert, Mary E., 1984– author.
Title: Family game night and other catastrophes / Mary E. Lambert.
Description: First edition. | New York, NY : Scholastic Press, 2017. | Summary: Seventh-grader Annabelle's mother is a hoarder, and their whole house is full of canned goods, broken toys, fabric, and old newspapers—but when a pile of newspapers (organized by weather reports) falls on Annabelle's younger sister Leslie and their mother is more concerned about the newspapers, it sets off a chain of events that brings their fix-it-all grandmother in and Annabelle realizes that if there is any hope for change she can not isolate herself and keep her family's problems secret.
Identifiers: LCCN 2016030472 (print) | LCCN 2016032690 (ebook) | ISBN 9780545931984 (hardcover) | ISBN 9780545932004
Subjects: LCSH: Compulsive hoarding—Juvenile fiction. | Obsessive-compulsive disorder—Juvenile fiction. | Family secrets—Juvenile fiction. | Mothers and daughters—Juvenile fiction. | Sisters—Juvenile fiction. | Families—Juvenile fiction. | CYAC: Compulsive hoarding—Fiction. | Obsessive-compulsive disorder—Fiction. | Secrets—Fiction. | Mothers and daughters—Fiction. | Sisters—Fiction. | Family problems—Fiction.
Classification: LCC PZ7.1.L25 Fam 2017 (print) | LCC PZ7.1.L25 (ebook) | DDC 813.6 [Fic] —dc23
LC record available at https://lccn.loc.gov/2016030472

10 9 8 7 6 5 4 3 2 1   17 18 19 20 21
Printed in the U.S.A.   23

First edition, March 2017
Book design by Abby Dening

This book is dedicated to my sister, Emily,
and to her border terrier, Ned.

To Ned,
because my sister believes the world would be better
if everyone had a dog like hers.

And to Emily,
because I know it would be better if everyone
had a sister like mine.

The newspapers fell on my sister at breakfast this morning.

And I didn't do anything to stop it.

Sometimes I have this feeling that I'm completely disconnected from my body, like I'm watching my life on TV or in a dream, and it doesn't occur to me until ten minutes or two weeks later that, hey, I could've done something. I don't have to sit in the audience and watch things fall apart.

But that's exactly what I did at breakfast. I just sat there, waiting to see if today would be the day the newspapers finally fell. It was the "highs in the mid to upper 70s" pile that came crashing down. The newspapers are organized by weather report, and since it's almost June, Mom has been adding to the "highs in the mid to upper 70s" pile every day. Lately she's had to stand on her tiptoes in order to reach the top, and this morning—before she could even add to it—it was already swaying from side to side, back and forth. It looked like a Jenga tower right before someone loses, and today Leslie was the loser.

I've known for weeks now that they were bound to come crashing down. It's why I haven't sat at the head of the table since spring break. The head of the table is the best seat in the house—it's closest to the fridge and, therefore, the fewest steps to the milk. Yes, I am that lazy. And, apparently, so is my sister, because as soon as I switched seats, she nabbed my old one. I should have warned her not to sit there, told her why I'd changed seats. But, honestly, it never occurred to me.

I thought about how the newspapers would probably fall on her head, and in cold, fatalistic silence, I consumed my cereal, morning after morning, waiting and watching.

I was on my last spoonful of Cocoa Krispies when it happened. The milk had just turned that perfect shade of brownish purple. Leslie was polishing off her Cheerios. Dad was eating his whole-wheat toast. And Mom was in bed or in the shower or on the sofa, doing whatever it is she does after making Dad's toast. Mom does leave the house every now and then, usually for trips to the grocery store when there's no one else to do it. But most of the time, she prefers to stay right where she is, thank you very much. And my brother, who never eats breakfast—at least not at home with us—had just raced out the door.

"Take me with you," I shouted at Chad as he breezed past, keys in hand.

"Denied," he said with a smile. Chad is never mean when he says no. He's never mean, period. He just isn't nice. I bet Chad doesn't even know my favorite color.

His is red.

"But it's the last day," I said. "I can be ready in two seconds. Please, please, let me come with you. I don't want to take the—"

Chad slammed the door before I could say "bus."

I don't know if he was upset about something or running late to pick up a friend or, maybe, he just couldn't wait to get out of the house. I can relate. Whatever his reason, when I say Chad slammed the door, I mean he slammed it. A real window-rattling, earthquake-imitating, neighbor-waking slam.

"That's okay, Annabelle," Leslie said to me, her back to the wobbling Jenga tower. "I like riding with you on the—"

The newspapers fell before Leslie could say "bus."

Crash.

Thud.

A hundred dusty, mildewy newspapers landed in Leslie's bowl of Cheerios and sent her spoon flying.

Fhwump.

More newspapers clobbered her on the back of the neck.

"Mwaaahhh." Leslie made a sound like a startled goat.

"What the—what's going on?" Dad looked up from his toast and, ironically enough, from the newspaper he was reading. He was just in time to see his youngest nearly decapitated. Death by periodical. What a way to go.

Thunk. The last newspaper fell.

I put down my spoon and glared at Dad, who had gotten up to pat Leslie's back and ask if she was okay. The beautiful brownish-purple milk in my cereal bowl would go to waste now. I wasn't about to drink it, even if it was chocolate flavored. Not with all the dust and newspaper bits floating around the room.

"What do you think is going on?" I said. "Chad knocked over Mom's newspapers when he slammed the door."

Dad didn't answer. He just sat back down and took a bite of toast. Dust and all. "This is awful," he said, and I couldn't tell if he meant the dirty toast or the newspapers falling on Leslie. Dad chewed, swallowed, and shook his head before setting his toast back on his plate. "That boy. I do hope he's careful on the road. He can be so reckless."

You're the reckless one, I wanted to shout. *You're the one who let Mom turn our kitchen into a death trap.* And the kitchen isn't even the worst room in the house. It makes me want to scream.

Instead, I sneezed.

I sneezed three more times as I carried my bowl from the

table to the kitchen sink and rinsed it out. We'll probably all die from inhaling newspaper dust full of some horrible airborne disease. Like hantavirus. If the piles of junk don't crush us to death first.

I guess I should have asked Leslie if she was all right, but I was too annoyed with Dad to say anything in front of him. He almost never puts his foot down with Mom.

I was still sneezing when Mom, summoned no doubt by the crash-thud-thunk of her collapsing newspapers, waddled into the room. She wore one of her colorful muumuus. Lime green with big orange flowers. You can always gauge Mom's mood by which muumuu she has on. Beware the pastels.

"What happened?" Her voice cut through the sound of the running water. I turned to watch Mom fly into the kitchen. It may not look like it, but Mom can really move when she wants to. "No! No, no, no," she said, rushing to Leslie's side. But instead of wrapping Leslie in her arms, she started gathering her newspapers.

"Which pile fell?" she demanded.

Thirteen hours, fifty-six minutes, and one last day
of school later, Leslie asks to sleep in my room. Not that I
blame her. It's the only clean room in the entire house.

A couple of years ago, on my tenth birthday, I went ber-
serk. The first half of the day was normal enough. We had
cake and ice cream at the picnic tables under the big cotton-
wood tree—Mom was too embarrassed to let guests in the
house, but staying outside didn't really bother me. We live a
little ways outside of town, and our yard is five acres. You
can't even see a neighbor's house from our place. So I was
happy to open presents and play Blind Man's Bluff and
charades out on the lawn. Then everyone went home, and I
carried my presents upstairs.

At the time, Mom's "collections" had slowly been taking over the house for a couple of years. It was gradual at first, so gradual that I didn't realize what was happening. The house had always been a little messy. But one day, Mom ran out of space in the hall cupboards and then, before I knew it, my bedroom was floor-to-ceiling color-coded piles of old and new towels, sheets, tablecloths, rags, and skirts and shirts and pants purchased at bargain prices with promises they would be hemmed or mended or taken in. They never were. And the piles kept growing.

It got so bad that I could barely walk through my bedroom. There were only small pathways through the fabric to my bed and my dresser. The desk and desk chair were completely buried. Between piles were the remnants of a life: my backpack, my schoolbooks, my scattered toys. I had to dig through sheets and towels whenever I wanted to find anything.

I didn't always hate it. Sometimes it felt like a treasure hunt. And sometimes it felt all cozy and safe and warm. Leslie and I would build nests in the fabric, burrow down and play there. Or read, swaddled deep in the sheets.

But on my tenth birthday, I snapped.

It was bright and sunny outside, but my room was dark and dim and much too soft. I've heard they lock crazy people in rooms like that, where everything is padded so they can't hurt themselves. And I knew that if I slept in that cotton-and-down-feather room one more night, I would need a padded cell of my own someday. I'd end up just like Mom.

I dropped all my new presents and crossed the room to open my window. I just wanted to let in a little light. Fresh air. Some of that outside, blue-sky freedom. But the moment I pried open my window, I knew it: Either Mom's fabric collection was going out the window or I was.

Without thinking, without planning, without permission, I started tossing everything out the window. At first it was kind of fun. The fabric would come unfurled midair and billow out, parachuting down in drifts. Some fabric got stuck in the cottonwood tree. But most of it reached the lawn, transforming the yard into a giant patchwork quilt.

Pink sheets. Blue towels. Green pillowcases. Orange and yellow shirts. Red pants. Purple skirts. Teal and butterfly fabric from a sewing project that never was. A pair of plaid boxers got stuck on an especially high branch of the cotton-wood tree. No one could reach them, so the boxers camped out there for weeks until a big storm finally blew them away.

And it wasn't just Mom's fabric collection that went out the window. I threw my own stuff outside, too. Even my brand-new presents. Anything nonessential had to go. Had to, had to, had to.

At some point, Mom noticed her fabric collection raining down on the side yard, and she started banging on my locked door, issuing cease and desist orders. I can still hear her fist hammering on the door, punctuated with screams: "Annabelle!" Bang, bang. "Annabelle Marie!" Bang, bang, bang. "Annabelle Marie Balog! Open this door!!!" Bang, bang. "Do you hear me?" Of course I heard, but I completely ignored her, and the harder she banged, the harder I threw. Then, just when I was certain Mom would hammer my door right off its hinges and ground me for seven eternities, Dad took my side. To my utter and complete astonishment, he actually put his foot down.

"The kids," I heard him say through the door, "have a right to control what's kept in their rooms."

But I didn't have the right to control anything else, and Mom's fabric collection didn't stay out on the lawn for long. As soon as I banished it from my room, Mom brought her precious linens back inside, where they took up residence on the couch and blocked off the living room window seat.

Ever since then I only allow things in my room that I use on a regular basis. Once a week, I clean out everything and throw away anything that I haven't used in the last seven days. Some people might think my bedroom is a little depressing. White walls. No decorations. The only exception is a little watercolor painting that's been hanging on my wall for as long as I can remember. But compared with the rest of our house, my room is wide-open spaces and fresh air. And I want to keep it that way. Which is why whenever Leslie asks to sleep in my room (and she asks a lot), I say no. I have to keep my space special, neat, and clean.

But tonight is different. I feel bad that I didn't warn Leslie about the newspapers, so when she asks, I give her permission to sleep in my room. Just this once. And I warn her: "If you leave anything in here, I'll throw it away."

She nods with this real solemn expression. "Thank you," she says.

Leslie's room is like a graveyard where dolls and stuffed animals and chunks of Fisher-Price plastic go to die. All the toys Mom drags home from yard sales and curbsides and Walmart bargain bins end up in Leslie's room. (Except for the Beanie Babies. Those are wedged between the banister rails all the way up the stairs.)

Last year my history teacher showed us pictures of the catacombs in Paris. Mr. Zimmer said that when the French people ran out of places to stick dead bodies, they started dumping the corpses in these big underground tunnels. And I swear, when Mr. Zimmer showed me those pictures of dark tunnels all piled up with skulls and thighbones, I thought of my sister's bedroom.

It's so awful that I'm always telling her: "You've got a window. Use it."

She never takes me up on my advice, even when I offer to help her. "Dad will back us up if we clean out your room," I say. "He has to, even if Mom won't like it." But Leslie won't let me do anything. She just shakes her head and mutters a halfhearted something about how "Mom was so mad" after I threw the sheets out my window.

At bedtime, when Leslie comes to my room with her arms full of stuff from the Toy Catacombs, I make her show me every single thing she wants to bring through that door. Every single thing. She has a pillow and a comforter. Those are approved. She has Bunbun, the stuffed rabbit she still sleeps with—a long time ago, I used to have one just like it. As far as I'm concerned, Bunbun is iffier, but I'm still willing to approve it. Last of all, she has a manila folder.

"What's that?" I ask. It's nonessential—the folder cannot stay.

She clutches the file to her chest. "I want to show you something."

I don't want to talk about her folder. I want to talk about Drew Benson and My Very Last Day of Seventh Grade. I can't bring school people home anymore. For obvious reasons, I keep them at least five miles away from my house at all times. I call this my Five-Mile-Radius Rule. So gossiping with Leslie is the next-best thing. But Leslie hugs the folder even more tightly and her eyes go all Bambi. The only difference between Leslie and Bambi is that Leslie's eyes are this really pretty shade of light green instead of brown. I know a lost cause when I see one. I sigh and plop down on the edge of my bed.

"All right," I say.

Leslie joins me. She doesn't notice any lack of enthusiasm on my part.

"Will you answer a question?" she asks.

"Maybe."

Leslie is quiet for a minute. Then she says, "What are you afraid of?"

Easy. It's so easy to answer that I don't even hesitate.

"Turning into Mom," I say.

"No." Leslie shakes her head. "I mean, what do you worry about?"

"Turning into Mom," I repeat.

"No," she says. Clearly, I'm not giving her the answer she wants. "I mean, what *scares* you?"

News flash, Leslie: The answer is still "turning into Mom." But instead of prolonging this fun little cycle, I turn the question around on her. "Why? What are you so scared of?"

Leslie pushes the manila folder into my hands.

I open it to find a stack of articles. Most are internet printouts, but one or two have obviously been clipped from magazines or newspapers.

HOARDER KILLED BY HIS OWN CLUTTER.

**WOMAN FOUND DEAD
AMID HUNDREDS OF TONS OF JUNK.**

12

MAN BURIED ALIVE UNDER RUBBLE
IN HIS OWN HOME.

"Gross!" I say, and slam the folder shut. There are at least a dozen stories in there. "Why do you even have this?"

Without meeting my eyes, Leslie shrugs.

I reopen the folder and start skimming the first article. ". . . an eighty-six-year-old woman was found crushed to death in her home last week. In addition to the mounds of garbage in the front rooms, the rear of the house was completely inaccessible. Family members said the rooms hadn't been usable in years . . ."

This is way too close to home. After all, Mom already shut down one of our rooms, the former dining room. In my head, I call it the Forbidden Room, because Mom locked it up one day and threw away the key. She won't say why she locked it or what's inside. But the not knowing drives me nuts. Nuts, nuts, nuts. I really do wonder what she's keeping in there. Today I'm leaning toward cornstarch. Mountains of it.

Whenever Mom and Dad have one of their bad fights (which isn't too often), Dad threatens to chop down the ex–dining room door or call the fire department to do it for him. Personally, I'd just call a locksmith, but Dad can be a total drama king when he's fighting with Mom. The rest of the time, he's pretty laid-back. Or maybe *oblivious* is a better word for it.

I shuffle to the next article in Leslie's folder and continue reading: ". . . an Ohio man who, among other things, kept dozens of dogs in his home, was found dead on Friday. The hungry canines had eaten . . ."

I slam the folder shut again.

"Are you trying to give me nightmares?"

"I already have nightmares," Leslie says to her hands. "Almost every night."

"Well, duh, you little dummy. I'd have nightmares, too, if I was reading this before bed."

She looks up, her Bambi eyes wide with surprise. We stare at each other and then, for some reason, we both burst out laughing. I throw the folder out in the hallway, which is already so full of stuff—mostly Mom's catalogue and junk-mail collections—that a few more papers will hardly make a difference.

"Hey," I say, "wanna sleep in my bed tonight? Instead of on the floor?"

Leslie nods.

We cuddle under the covers and I finally get to tell her about holding hands with Drew in the hall between classes and about Rae's party tomorrow night. Drew's going to be there.

He sat next to me and Rae in science this year. Then sometime around spring break, he started eating lunch with us—it was after I stopped him from accidentally burning down the school (rubbing alcohol+Bunsen burner=Max's idea of a prank on Drew that would have gone horribly, horribly wrong). Tomorrow will be the first time I've hung out with him outside of school, and I can't tell Leslie about it without smiling. I'm lying there in bed beside her, smiling so wide my cheeks hurt.

Then Leslie tells me about the new kid in her class—the one who started school when there were only three days left in the year. Who does that? Leslie says he just moved here and wanted to make some friends for the summer. But I think he sounds weird.

We giggle about nothing. She slaps my arm, and I pinch her leg. After a while we get really quiet, the way people do just before they fall asleep. I say, "I hope it didn't hurt too much when the newspapers fell on you. I wish things were different around here."

Leslie doesn't answer. I think she's already asleep.

I love, love, love going to Rae's house. Every time I walk inside, I feel like I'm stepping into a magazine. Mrs. McKinley keeps fresh flowers on the dining room table. Over the mantle, there's a framed painting—a real, one-of-a-kind, signed-by-the-artist painting from a gallery in New York City. The books on the shelves are alphabetized, and everything— the furniture, the throw pillows, the curtains—it all matches. Rae said her mom actually hired someone to help decorate. Even before my mom started "collecting," our house wasn't half as nice as Rae's.

I'll never forget the first time Rae invited me over. It was the middle of fifth grade, not too long after my tenth birthday. Her family had just moved to Colorado from Maryland,

and not only was her house perfect, but her mom fed us homemade cookies and her big sister gave us manicures. I thought families like Rae's, with houses that perfect, only existed in books or TV shows. And that's when I knew Rae and I were meant to be best friends.

So I was excited that the end-of-the-year party was at Rae's house. And even better, Mrs. McKinley let us invite guys for the first half. We asked Drew and some of Drew's friends—Joey and Thomas.

I get to the McKinleys' house first. A few minutes later, when our friends Melanie and Jenny show up, Rae hands out water balloons and says, "Follow me." She leads us into the hedge that lines the McKinleys' driveway and we hide there, waiting and watching . . .

My heart is racing a million miles a minute. I guess my future as a spy is out. Evidently, ambushing a couple of guys with water balloons is all the excitement I can handle. When Joey and Thomas's ride pulls up, Rae yells, "Now!" and the four of us jump out of the bushes screaming at the top of our lungs and pelting the guys with water balloons. Two of my balloons hit their targets, but Joey and Thomas are already wearing their swimsuits, so it really doesn't matter if we soak them.

Still, I feel so good about my role in the ambush that I'm rethinking my future as a spy.

"Ha! James Bond better watch out!" I shout. There's so

17

much noise that no one hears my brag, which is a good thing, because as the words leave my mouth, I trip and land on my third balloon, soaking myself.

While I scramble to my feet and give thanks no one noticed my fall, Joey nabs Melanie's last water balloon. He tosses it at Rae, who squeals and runs around the side of her house. Thomas, Joey, and Melanie follow, yelling things like "You're so dead!"

Jenny is even unluckier than me—she doesn't get nailed by her own balloon. It's worse than that. As Joey's dad climbs out of the car, one of her balloons smacks him in the chest, exploding all over his suit and the sandwich he's eating. I don't know why he's driving around with a submarine sandwich, but I doubt he'll finish it now.

Jenny and I gasp at the same time.

"Oh my gosh! I'm so sorry," she says, her hands covering her mouth.

"My sandwich," says Joey's dad in a sad voice.

Mrs. McKinley must have seen it all from the window, because she comes running from the house, holding a towel and apologizing. Jenny's face turns as bright red as her hair, and she slinks back in the bushes to hide or pout or something.

I think about going after her, but I don't know what to say and I don't want to be hiding in the bushes when Drew arrives, so I start picking up all the little balloon bits that are now scattered across the lawn. I've heard birds can choke on them. After Joey's dad drives away—minus one soggy sandwich—Mrs. McKinley starts helping me pick up the broken water balloons.

So I'm alone with Rae's mom when the last two cars pull up. Amanda and Drew arrive at the same time.

"What's in your hand?" Drew asks after climbing out of his car.

I show him the balloon fragments and say, "You're just lucky you didn't get here when Thomas and Joey did. I had a balloon with your name on it."

He laughs and helps us pick up the last few bits of neon balloon. Then I take him around the side of the house, and we join the others who are already swimming. Amanda doesn't come with us. She catches a glimpse of Jenny's hair and stops to ask why she's hiding.

A little while later, Amanda and Jenny join the rest of us, and everything is fine . . . until Leslie's first text comes at 7:32 p.m., just as everyone is finishing their pizza and getting back in the pool.

"Let's play water basketball," says Joey, shoving a huge wad of crust into his mouth. I don't know what Melanie sees in him, but she's had a crush on Joey for weeks now.

"What are you waiting for?" says Thomas, and he does

a cannonball into the pool, splashing all of us and soaking my last bite. There's a bunch of squealing, and three or four more people, including Joey and Melanie, jump in after him.

That's when my phone buzzes. I set my chlorinated pizza back on its paper plate and dry my hands before plucking it from a pile of towels.

"C'mon, Drew! Aren't you gonna play with us?" Joey calls from the water as I glance down at Leslie's text. It says:

Dad found my articles. He's really upset.

Great. Just great. Now Dad knows about the File o' Death. This will not go over well.

"Nah," Drew answers Joey. "I'm not getting back in the water unless everyone else does." He's looking at me.

I get a little fluttery feeling in my stomach, and suddenly I'm annoyed that Leslie is texting me. I don't want to think about nightmares and Death Files. There's an endless summer, trapped in the house of Toy Catacombs and ex–dining rooms, ahead of us. On the rare, special days when I'm away from it all, I don't want to drag my problems with me. I want to forget them. Sometimes forgetting things is the only way to be happy.

"But I need you on my team," says Thomas. "We'll get creamed without you."

"Hey," says Rae, who is standing at his elbow. "I'm not

that bad." (She is.) Rae throws a bunch of water in Thomas's face and starts a splash war.

I look back at the message. I don't want this. Not now. I want to play water basketball and join the splash fight. I want to stay up late watching movies and eating cookie dough. And maybe, if Mrs. McKinley goes to bed early enough, I want to sneak out with the other girls and TP someone's house. Rae has a bunch of toilet paper hidden under her bed. Just in case.

I look up from my phone. Drew is still standing there. His head is tilted to one side, like he's waiting for the answer to a question he hasn't asked yet.

"Is something wrong?" he says.

Yes! My mom stores so much junk in our house that my sister thinks it's going to kill her. She might not be wrong. But I can't tell Drew that. None of my friends know, and I plan to keep it that way. I have to keep it that way. I'm not going to be that girl, the one everyone feels sorry for, the one with the disgusting house and the creepy mom.

"It's fine." I toss my phone back into the pile of towels.

"You in?" He gestures toward the pool.

"Yeah." I race past him and jump into the water. When I surface, he's already in the pool. I kick off the side and race him to see who can steal the ball from Joey first. I win. (But part of me wonders if it's because he didn't try very hard.)

The next text comes at 8:12 p.m., around the time we're just settling down to watch *Friday the 13th*.

I told Dad about my nightmares. I think it was a mistake.

I ignore the text. I don't like scary movies and am busy trying to convince Rae that we should watch something else, but Rae promises that *Friday the 13th* is "from, like, 1980 so it's super cheesy." I disagree. It's not cheesy; it's terrifying. I start chewing my thumbnail in the very first scene. It only gets worse, and when Annie is being chased through the woods, I freak out and try to dive into the couch cushion at my back. Only I miss the couch cushion. Drew is sitting a lot closer than I realized. I whack my head on his shoulder.

"Are you okay?" We say it at the same time.

"I'm fine." We speak in unison again, and we're both laughing like huge dorks when Annie's throat gets slit.

"Be quiet. Some of us are trying to watch the movie," says Melanie. She throws a handful of popcorn at me and Drew.

"Don't!" says Rae. "Mom will kill me if you get grease on her couch."

I try to smother my laughter as I clutch my head where it collided with Drew's shoulder. It actually does hurt a little, but I completely forget any pain when Drew puts an arm around me. "I don't really like scary movies either," he whispers.

He doesn't just say it to be nice. I can feel him flinch every time someone else is axed or macheted or impaled. I don't think Mrs. McKinley knows we're watching this, but

22

it's a great excuse to lean in closer to Drew. I feel like I could sit here forever, surrounded by friends and popcorn and Drew's arm.

So I can't do it. I can't make myself move or get up from the couch or even reply when Leslie's next text comes, at 8:34 p.m.:

Mom and Dad are fighting. I think it's my fault.
What should I do?

Again at 8:47 p.m.:

Dad said the d-word. I don't know what to do.

And again at 8:52 p.m.:

Please call me.

After that, Melanie complains all the buzzing is ruining the movie. So I hold down the button until the screen turns black, feeling guilty that I'm so happy for an excuse to turn off my phone. I don't know what to tell Leslie, and tonight I don't want to be part of the drama at home. I just couldn't quite seem to turn it off on my own.

My phone is still off after the movie ends and Rae's mom makes the boys go home. I walk Drew out front when his mom calls to say she's almost to the McKinleys' house. He's the last of the guys, and it's just the two of us on the driveway. We're far enough away from any city lights that the entire night sky sparkles. My head is tilted back and I'm watching the stars when Drew says: "Hey, we should hang out this summer."

A little thrill runs down my spine. I stop looking at the stars and turn toward him. This is the best news . . . but it's also the worst news, and I hate that I have to choose my next words carefully. "That would be cool," I say. "Maybe we can meet in town somewhere." I'll meet him anywhere. As long as it's at least five miles away from home. Luckily for me, his ride pulls up before he can say anything about going over to each other's houses.

My phone is still off when Jenny, Melanie, Rae, Amanda, and I play Truth or Dare. I'm not a big fan of Truth or Dare, but I'm lucky again. I don't have to lie about my mom or my house. They're all too interested in asking me questions about Drew. Only Amanda asks a different question. She wants to know if *Pinocchio* is still my favorite Disney movie. It is. I know it's a weird choice, but for some reason, there was just something I always really liked about that wooden puppet and the carver who loves him so much.

Since my questions were all so easy, I feel kind of bad when Melanie double-dog dares Amanda to jump in the pool *naked*.

I don't think Amanda exactly wants to do it but she says okay anyway.

Amanda takes people by surprise sometimes. She's quiet and dreamy and, honestly, a little different. She notices the things other people miss, and she can be talked into doing the craziest stuff. I think it's because Amanda doesn't actually care what people think of her. But at the same time, I know she really, really wants people to like her. Who doesn't?

We all troop outside, and I stand at the end of the pool. This time I don't look up at the stars. I stare at the rippling water and imagine myself saying: *Hey, Amanda, you don't have to do this. It's a stupid game. We'll still be your friends if you don't.*

I'm still staring at the water, trying to make the words come out, when I hear a splash. The other girls are shrieking, and I see Amanda's clothes in a heap near one of the lounge chairs. A dark shape moves in the water. It's pitch-black, since we haven't turned on any lights—Mr. and Mrs. McKinley might not like this game.

I just stand there, laughing along with everyone else when Amanda shouts, "It's cold!!!" Jenny tosses her a towel as she climbs out of the water. Amanda laughs along with the rest of us and wraps herself tightly in the towel. But I'm not quite comforted. There are a lot of kinds of laughter.

My phone is still off when everyone else falls asleep, and Rae and I are the only ones awake. It feels like we're the only two people in the entire world. I start to nod off a couple of times, but Rae won't let me. We decide it will be too much work to TP someone's house, so we sneak into the kitchen. It's around 4:30 a.m., and we're both slaphappy and sleep-deprived, which is probably why we decide it's the perfect time to make pancakes. I start to pull out the just-add-water mix Mrs. McKinley keeps in the cupboard by the griddle, but Rae stops me. "Let's invent a recipe," she says.

This is when I like Rae best—when it's just the two of us. Rae seems to agree. She says: "Think how jealous everyone will be when they find out we stayed up without them."

"Yeah," I say.

Rae starts digging around in her mom's spice rack.

"You can't make fun of me if I tell you something," she says.

"I won't."

"Sometimes I think I want to be a cook when I grow up."

"Why would I laugh at that?"

She sets the nutmeg and cinnamon on the counter with a shrug. "I usually tell people I want to be a lawyer or a doctor or something important."

"What's more important than food?"

That's when I get the idea that if Rae wants to be a professional chef, she should learn to crack an egg with one hand. Like the chefs on TV. We watch a YouTube video, and the girl makes it look so easy that I'm confident we'll both get it right on the first try. But I'm overconfident, and even though I've cracked about a thousand eggs, I slam the egg against the side of the bowl way too hard. The shell shatters and my entire hand is coated in egg vomit. I run to the sink and scrub for a good sixty seconds.

Rae has better luck. Her shell cracks cleanly, but she can't separate the two halves of the shell to release the yolk. She drops it, shell and all, into the bowl. I don't try again. I'm not about to risk salmonella. So I sit on the counter and offer helpful advice while she goes through about a dozen eggs. We finally give up, pick the shell out of one of the eggs, and make the rest of the batter.

The pancakes are terrible—way too much cinnamon. Also they're undercooked and full of eggshell. The syrup sticks to the roof of my mouth, making it difficult to swallow. And for some reason, my stomach hurts. I probably ate too much cookie dough and popcorn during the movie.

By 10:00 a.m., I'm eating another round of pancakes. Rae's mom cooked these, so they're not runny in the middle and there's no eggshell. It doesn't make me feel any better, though. I'm grouchy. My stomach still hurts, and I'm only half-awake. So I don't say much—especially once everyone starts in on their parents.

Rae's parents and older sister are safely outside, drinking coffee on the back deck, which means it's just our friends when it starts.

"My mom is making me take some pottery class." Jenny rolls her eyes. "She thinks the internet is rotting my brain and art class is going to be 'so much fun.' Like my mom's not constantly online. She should worry about her own brain."

28

"Well, my parents are dragging us all to Family Camp, which is way worse," Melanie says. "It lasts an entire week, and it's so embarrassing. Every time we go up there, my dad wears all these lame T-shirts and my mom brings her fanny pack."

"Does the camp have horses?" Jenny asks. She's completely horse-obsessed.

Melanie rolls her eyes. "Who cares?"

Rae is laughing. "I know exactly which shirts you're talking about. Doesn't your dad have one with something about Velcro on it?"

Melanie groans. "Yeah. It says, 'Velcro—what a rip off!'"

"Wait. Why is that supposed to be funny?" says Jenny.

"It's not funny. That's my point," Melanie says.

I wash down a mouthful of syrup and pancake with a big gulp of milk. I think about explaining the pun to Jenny, but I'm too tired and I don't want to get dragged into this conversation. I wish my problems could be summed up with embarrassing T-shirts and fanny packs.

"Who cares what your dad wears?" Rae asks. "As long as he lets you wear what you want. I bought this really cute bikini to sunbathe in when we're at the lake house, and my dad said I had to return it."

"Ugh, I hate how everyone's leaving," says Jenny. "When do you go?"

"I think early Friday," says Rae.

I silently agree with Jenny. I hate how Rae and her family leave for almost half the summer every year. It's so depressing when she's gone.

"I told you your parents wouldn't like that swimsuit," Melanie says, returning to the main point. "It was pretty scandalous."

"Was not," Rae says.

Melanie and Rae start arguing about the bikini, then Jenny says something about how her mom almost didn't let her come to the sleepover because she heard that guys were invited . . . and it goes on from there.

Curfews. Dating. Grades. Allowances.

Complaining about parents is sort of like an Olympic sport. But I don't compete. The kids with real problems never do. I hear the same things at school all the time. "My mom's such a jerk. She made me go to bed before the movie was over" or "I hate my dad. He wouldn't let me go out because it was a school night." But you almost never hear the other stuff. "Mom was drunk again." Or "Dad didn't have the money for bail." Or "My mom saves all her fingernail clippings in old baby food jars."

Even Dad thinks that one is weird.

But, to tell the truth, Dad isn't much better than Mom. He teaches English literature at the community college and calls himself "a Sherlock Holmes aficionado." He spends half his life sitting in his den, wearing his deerstalker hat and

30

fiddling with his pipe, which he only smokes when things are really, really intense. The worse Mom gets, the more time he spends in the nineteenth century with Dr. Watson.

Amanda is the only other person at the table who doesn't complain. She barely looks up from her pancakes, just keeps eating like she's a starved woman.

I wonder what her damage is.

Chad picks me up around noon. Leslie can be kind of high-strung, so I haven't been as worried as I could have been until Chad's ancient truck comes rattling up the drive. He would never volunteer to pick me up, which means Dad made him, which means Leslie's Death Files succeeded where the collapse of a hundred newspapers failed. Something must have pulled Dad into the present. I'm sure it will be a temporary condition. But it's enough to make me wonder if the fight last night was worse than I thought.

Rae walks me out to Chad's truck. I throw my sleeping bag and overnight sack in the back and hop in the passenger seat, waving goodbye as we cruise toward the open road.

It's one of the Glorious Days.

I don't say that out loud. If I said those kinds of thoughts out loud, people might not understand. It's the sort of thing Amanda sometimes says and then Melanie and Rae make faces at each other behind her back. But in my head, I call days like this Glorious Days.

31

Deep blue sky. Fluffy white clouds. Early summer so the grass and trees are still that bright-alive shade of green. Glorious. While we drive, I watch the cloud shadows drift over meadows and collide with the Rocky Mountains. Seriously, the drive home from Rae's house looks like an advertisement for the Colorado Tourism Office. How can it be so beautiful out here when inside everything is such a mess?

Chad and I don't talk at first. I can't decide which question to ask, and even if I could decide, I'm not sure I want to hear the answer. So instead I roll down my window, put my feet on the dash, turn my face toward the sun, and doze. Chad flips through radio stations for a while. When he can't find anything to settle on, I shift in my seat and open my eyes.

"Were you home last night?"

"Nope," he says.

"Out partying?"

He flashes a quick grin. "You could say that." Melanie's and Jenny's parents might have super strict curfews, but I don't think it's ever occurred to Mom and Dad to set one for any of us.

"Do you think it was bad?"

"Leslie does."

"Yeah, but Leslie calls it a fight if you burp and forget to say excuse me." I pull out my phone and force myself to turn it on. I scroll through her texts. "She keeps saying they were using the d-word."

"Which one?" asks Chad. Like he doesn't know. "Dreamy?"

I roll my eyes. Chad keeps going.

"Dynamic? Daring? Dazzling?"

"Now you're just listing words you wish people would use to describe you."

"Oh, it's what the people say about me."

Even though I'm stressed out and worried, I laugh. This encourages Chad, who says, "Although, knowing Dad, it was probably something British-sounding."

"What about dodgy?"

"Good one. Or dimwit. Or divvy. Or duffer."

"Show-off," I say, laughing a little more. We're quiet for another minute before I finally ask: "Do you think they'll really get divorced this time?"

Chad shakes his head. "No, the parents might fight it out every now and then, but they've gotta know that neither of them will ever find anyone else who can put up with them."

Call me a romantic, but I think this is Chad's way of saying that he thinks our parents still love each other. After all, what is love if not putting up with someone else? Putting up with them through thick and thin. And our parents have put up with each other through a lot of thicks and thins. Forget love; sometimes when Dad holds Mom's hand while they watch the news, or when Mom slices Dad's toast for him even though he's perfectly capable of doing it himself, I think our parents still actually like each other.

And it's not as if this has never happened before. Every now and then, Dad notices that the house has metamorphosed into a giant storage shed for Mom's garbage and that we still can't get into the Forbidden Room. I really do wonder what she's keeping in there. The world's largest bottle-cap collection?

And whenever Dad does suddenly notice that our house should be declared a National Disaster, he starts throwing around all these royal decrees. Usually, it's something along the lines of: "If you don't clean out the house and unlock that door, we're through. I'm getting the kids out of here."

It's all very imperial of him. But what can you expect from someone who spends all day teaching books from a hundred years ago? Unfortunately, we all, even Mom, know that the drama king is full of empty threats. Well . . . Leslie might not have figured it out yet.

After a day or two of issuing proclamations, King Richard disappears and Dad resurfaces. He goes back to sipping Darjeeling tea and reading E. M. Forster, blissfully unaware that the view from his room has been blocked off by about a million cans of Bush's baked beans. (Mom uses his den to store her canned-foods collection.)

Chad stumbles across a song he likes on the radio and turns up the volume. I play with my phone, trying to decide if I should text Leslie. I end up texting Rae and Melanie and Drew instead. Three different times, I start to write Leslie a message, but nothing sounds quite right, and before I can decide on anything, we're turning up the gravel drive to our house. Everything looks the same, just the way I left it yesterday, and I succeed in convincing myself that Chad is right. Mom and Dad aren't getting a divorce. The fight last night was all a part of their routine. As usual, Leslie was overreacting.

This feeling lasts until I walk in the front door and trip over a can of Bush's baked beans.

I'm **still flat** on my back when Dad comes crashing out of the den, briefcase on his shoulder and red suitcase in hand. Canned vegetables scatter in his wake. The suitcase wheels keep getting caught on the cans, but Dad just yanks on the handle, sending the bag airborne. My father, the spacey, mild-mannered professor, is in the middle of a full-fledged, royal tantrum. I blink up at him.

"Oh, hello there, Annabelle," Dad says, and his suitcase lands a few inches away from the spot where I fell. "I didn't realize you were home. How was the party?"

I stay on my butt and blink up at him. Our entryway looks like the canned-goods aisle of a grocery store after a major earthquake. And he wants want to know how the party was?

"Dad, what's going on?"

He glances toward our blocked-off parlor window. "Oh, nothing much. I'm just off for the UK tour." Dad takes a group of community college students around England, Scotland, and Wales every summer. Their first stop is always 221B Baker Street. The Sherlock Holmes Museum in London. You'd think they would head for Westminster Abbey or Buckingham Palace first. But not if my dad is your tour guide.

"I thought that wasn't until next week."

"Yes, well . . ." He shifts slightly from foot to foot. I might not have noticed his fidgeting except, for some reason, I haven't picked myself up from the floor yet. I sit there and watch him squirm. "I thought I would head over a little early this year. It'll give me some time to do a little research for a paper I'm writing."

"Since when?"

"It was a snap decision," he says. Then he sighs and squats down next to me. "You might as well know. Your mother and I had a little tiff last night."

I snort. I can't help it. Anything that would end in canned vegetables scattered everywhere has to be a lot more serious than "a little tiff." My mom might be a neurotic collector, but she is also neurotically systematic. Everything in our house has its place, its proper pile, its own room assignment. And the canned vegetables are always stacked like store displays in Dad's den.

"—we had a little tiff," Dad repeats firmly, as though I hadn't snorted at him. "And I decided it would be for the best if I left on my trip sooner than planned. Your mother knows what I expect of her while I'm gone. Try to help her out, Annabelle. She hasn't learned to let things go like you have."

"Does Chad know you're leaving?" I ask, feeling betrayed that he didn't say anything while we were in his truck.

Dad shakes his head. "Your mother and Leslie know, but I haven't spoken with Chad yet. Where is he?"

"Putting the truck in the garage. He said he was gonna check the oil or something."

A horn honks from outside. I look through the dusty windows that surround our front door. I can just make out a blurry green car in the drive.

"Ride's here," Dad says. "I'll stop by the garage and speak to Chad on my way out." He pulls himself up from his squat. He grunts a little, and I hear his knees pop. "I'll see you in a few weeks." He doesn't offer me a hand up.

"Wait, when?" I ask. "When are you coming home?"

Dad doesn't answer. He's already out the front door.

I stand, dust off my shorts, and take my stuff upstairs, wondering if this really is the end of Mom and Dad's marriage.

I wish we could go back to the way we were before.

— — —

I go right past Leslie's bedroom. Her door is closed, which is unusual. She doesn't like being shut up in the Toy Catacombs. I think about checking on her. But I can't. Not now. I have something I have to do first. Have to, have to, have to. During the school year, I do it every day as soon as I get home. In the summers, I only do it if I've gone somewhere. If Dad ever remembers his promise to take me on his UK tour, I'll need to bribe Leslie or Chad into helping me. Oh, who am I kidding? Of course Leslie would help me. Bribe or no bribe.

Once I close the door to my room (unlike Leslie, I keep my door closed as often as possible), I start by unpacking from the sleepover, careful to put everything in its proper place. Then I walk the perimeter of my room in a clockwise direction, starting at the door. I walk with my feet as close to the wall as possible. When I reach a piece of furniture, I walk around it, still remaining as close to the wall as I can. The furniture always slows me down, because that's where I have to check the most closely.

I reach the desk first. I open each drawer, examining it for anything new, anything I haven't personally put in there. Then I have to look under the desk, under the chair cushion, and, most important, behind the desk. When I first started the ritual, I didn't think to check behind the desk, and by the time it finally occurred to me, there were already fifteen or twenty *Real Simple* magazines wedged back there.

I reach the bed next and go through the same thing, remembering to lift the mattress. That's another place I've found old papers piling up. Then I check the nightstand, the dresser, and the closet.

I know it makes me sound a little crazy, and I haven't exactly told anyone about my system. But what's one more secret in a house piled up with them? And the ritual is necessary. It keeps my room clean.

See, when I was younger and stupider, I wasn't quite as careful as I am now and a few weeks after my tenth birthday, I noticed things were starting to pile up in my room again. It wasn't obvious at first. I would bring clean laundry up to my room, and there would be color-coordinated clothes that didn't belong to me tucked in the pile. A couple of pieces of junk mail would, somehow, navigate their way onto my desk.

My room slid from pristine to comfortably messy and, before I caught on, it was getting cluttered again. That's when I realized that rather than a head-on confrontation, Mom was using stealth. My room—all that lovely empty space— had to be filled. She's like a goldfish growing to the size of its bowl.

So I purged my room again. This second time, I carried it out in trash bags rather than sending it out the window. After that, I started checking my room on a daily basis.

On this particular sweep, I don't find anything, which makes me even more nervous about whatever went down last night. If Mom didn't take advantage of the fact that I was gone for over twelve hours to at least tuck a candy wrapper under my desk, then things must have been bad. Really bad.

Just as I am finishing the ritual, Leslie's voice interrupts me.

"Oh good, you're home," she says, appearing in my doorway. She looks awful, like she got even less sleep last night than I did. "Annabelle, I think I made a huge mistake."

"Leslie, it's not your fault that Dad left early for his trip."

"That's not what I mean," she says. "It's worse than that. Much worse."

What could be worse than Dad leaving?

I just stand there like an idiot, staring at Leslie and trying to figure out what on earth she's saying. Being tired makes me slow.

The skin around Leslie's eyes has turned this horrid purply-gray color. Neither one of us is a pretty crier. Whenever either of us cries, we turn into these horrible, puffy-eyed zombies. So I don't cry. But Leslie is younger, and she doesn't have very good control over her emotions.

"What happened?" I ask.

"Didn't you get my texts?"

"I might have seen a couple." I shrug. "But, you know how

it is. We were swimming and watching movies and I had my phone off for most of the night."

"But you never turn off your phone."

Guilt makes me blurt out a dumb excuse: "Well, all my friends were at the party. It's not like I was expecting to hear from anyone important."

Leslie winces. I want to pull the words back.

"I didn't mean—" I start trying to explain, but at the rate that today is going, I'll end up in China before I stop digging a deeper hole. "Never mind," I say. "Just tell me what's wrong." I can almost guarantee that whatever happened, Leslie has already found a way to blame herself.

She was born with a conscience the size of Alaska. Sometimes I wonder how she doesn't collapse under the weight of it. Personally, I think Jiminy Cricket is an awesome conscience. He's small. Portable. Easy to squash. I think most of us have a conscience that's sized something like an insect. But every now and then, a Leslie is born—someone who makes it a little harder for the rest of us to squash our crickets.

"Everything's wrong," says Leslie. "I never should have told Dad those articles belonged to me. At first he thought they were Mom's."

"Why did you tell him, then?"

"He asked." Leslie says this as if it explains everything.

And actually, it does. It wouldn't occur to Leslie that she could lie. Really, she's the sister who should love *Pinocchio*. But, no, her favorite old Disney movie is *Sleeping Beauty*.

"Listen," I say, "Dad is not going to divorce Mom. And even if he does, it's not your fault. This is about them and their problems." Their many, many problems.

"But I'm the one who left the folder in the hall."

"No, I'm the one who left it there. I threw it out of my room."

"But I told Dad about my nightmares. That's what made him so angry."

"Did he ask you about that, too?"

"Well, yes, but—"

"And you had to answer him, didn't you?" The good thing about Leslie having a conscience the size of Alaska is that it makes her really easy to manipulate.

"I guess . . ."

"Then it's not your fault."

"But . . . it is my fault that Grandma Nora's coming."

I've never been electrocuted, but I bet I know exactly how it feels. A shock runs through your body, and your chest gets tight. You can't breathe for a second, and your stomach turns into a massive knot and then, when it uncurls, you feel queasy and singed.

"What do you mean?"

"I called her." Leslie is speaking in a whisper now.

44

"You didn't."

Leslie nods.

"Why?" I have to ask. "What were you thinking?"

"I—It's just that—You weren't answering my texts and Chad was out and I was all alone and Mom and Dad were fighting and it was really bad. I didn't know what else to do."

Of course Leslie would turn to Grandma Nora. There's not really anyone else, and Grandma Nora is one of those Women Who Fix Things. She even tries to fix things that aren't broken. Like me.

"There's always room for improvement," Grandma Nora will say. It's practically her motto. She also likes to talk about Being an Independent Woman. When my mom and her sister were little kids, their dad (Grandma Nora's first husband) died, and Grandma Nora raised them on her own until she married her second husband. I can remember him. We called him Grandpa George, even though we weren't technically related. But then he died, too, and Grandma Nora was on her own again. So she's her own favorite example of an Independent Woman.

Her second-favorite example of an Independent Woman is my aunt Jill. Aunt Jill never got married and she doesn't have any kids, but she does have Degrees and a Career. She's a big-shot real estate agent. Or something like that. I don't think she sells homes. I think she sells things like warehouses and office buildings.

But whatever Aunt Jill does, she must get paid a ton of money, because every now and then my mom makes these really bitter comments about how rich her sister is. My family's not poor, but we can't afford to vacation on the Riviera or drive around in a Mercedes-Benz. Grandma Nora likes to remind us that Aunt Jill's is a convertible.

"Grandma Nora can't come," I tell Leslie. "We've got to stop her."

"Don't you think she'll help? She said she would take care of everything." Leslie says this in such a small voice that it's obvious even she knows it's a ridiculous suggestion. It doesn't matter how much you love sunshine and rainbows and unicorns, even an eternal optimist like Leslie can recognize Armageddon approaching.

I can't remember the last time Grandma Nora and Mom had a phone conversation without ending up in a fight, never mind that the last time Grandma Nora visited our house Grandpa George was with her. I'm not sure how many years it's been since he died. It feels like forever. At least four or five.

Everyone loved Grandpa George, especially Mom. He had all these silly nicknames for us, like he always called me Annabelle Lee, and then he would start reciting part of some old poem. Or sometimes he would call me Banana-belle. And Mom was always Polly or Pollywog or Paulina or Pauleeta. Anything but our real names.

Grandpa George was super laid-back compared with

Grandma Nora and Aunt Jill. He always talked about how great it was that Mom wanted to stay home to take care of her kids. He never dropped hints like Grandma Nora did about how Mom should get a "real job" once all her kids were in school. And he always asked about Mom's art. She used to paint these really pretty watercolors, and sometimes the one coffee shop in Chatham would put them on display.

She doesn't do that anymore. I haven't seen her paint anything in years. A couple of times a year Dad asks her when she's going to start again, or he'll bring home new brushes or special paper. It never makes any difference.

Grandma Nora has no idea how bad it's gotten around here. We do still see her occasionally. Once a year or so, Grandma Nora will have a fit of family togetherness, and she'll keep threatening to visit until Mom puts her off by agreeing to meet her in some nowhere town halfway between our two states. Sometimes Grandma Nora hints that she'd like to bring Aunt Jill along, but Mom absolutely, positively refuses to go if her sister will be there. I can't see how Aunt Jill would make things any worse. The family togetherness always follows the same miserable pattern. It starts with Grandma Nora giving me and Chad and Leslie hugs and kisses, but it ends in screaming matches and tears.

I'm not exactly sure why Mom and Grandma Nora hate each other so much, I just know that it's been that way ever since Grandpa George died. Dad always shoos the kids out as soon as they start fighting. I think Dad might be the only reason Mom and Grandma Nora haven't murdered each other yet. And now Grandma Nora is coming. To our house. And Mom doesn't know. And Dad is on his way out of the country.

"Maybe I can talk Grandma Nora out of coming," I tell Leslie.

"Too late."

"What?"

"Her plane already left."

I let out a massive groan. Only an Independent Woman Who Fixes Things would be flying halfway across the country already. It's been less than a full day since Leslie called. I grab my sister's arm. "Come on."

"Where are we going?" she asks as I drag her with me.

"To warn Mom."

It might be too late to stop the apocalypse, but maybe we can contain it.

I drag Leslie down the stairs, past the Beanie Babies and past the locked doors of the Forbidden Room. I really do wonder what she's keeping in there. All our old pencils and dried-up pens?

I pull Leslie toward the sound of cans being restacked. When we reach the den, I drop her arm and we pause to watch Mom. She's so involved with her can-tacular disaster that she doesn't notice us.

She looks terrible. She looks worse than Leslie, the puffy, purple-eyed monster. Did Mom even bother to shower this morning? Somehow I doubt it. I shower at least once a day, sometimes two or three times. Mom doesn't bathe that often, and today she's looking especially ripe.

Her wispy hair is pulled back with a clip. I can never decide what color her hair is. Leslie's hair is a really pretty chestnut-brown color. Mine is just a little lighter. But what do you call something that's not blond or brown or gray? Mom's hair is some depressing combination of all three. I almost talked her into dyeing it once last summer, but she wimped out. Mom can't handle change.

A few limp strands of her colorless hair are plastered to her forehead, and there are sweat stains as big as my face soaking through the armpits of her pink muumuu. Her pastel-pink muumuu.

"Do you want help?" Leslie asks, and Mom gives a little start. She pauses from restacking her cans to look over at us.

I literally grab my right hand with my left to stop myself from walloping Leslie upside the head. What is she thinking? Hasn't she noticed Mom's outfit? Doesn't she know what pastels mean? If nothing else, Leslie should know that offering to help Mom *put things back* is like asking a kid if he wants candy for dinner. It's not good for him, but he's not going to care.

"You look like you could use a hand," Leslie says when

49

Mom doesn't answer right away. "We'll help you, won't we, Annabelle?" Leslie's eyes are doing the Bambi Thing again. I really hate that stupid deer.

I don't want to spend the rest of the morning babysitting Mom. I want to do my duty by warning her about Grandma Nora, and then I want—no, I need—a nap. I break eye contact with my sister the fawn, only to accidentally meet Mom's eyes. They're red.

I'm tough. I can be as heartless as I need to be. That's what it takes to survive life in this house. Only, this morning I'm not quite tough enough.

"Sure, we'll help." I say it with all the enthusiasm of a martyr.

"Thanks, girls," Mom says.

It's quiet while we work, just the clinking of the cans and the swish-swish sound when I rub the grit off my hands and onto my shorts. From time to time, Mom interrupts with directions: Sort cans of the same fruit or vegetable by brand, larger cans on the bottom, labels facing out, cans with unusual contents go in their own special section, which is alphabetized and includes things like canned bread and pork brains in milk gravy. Gross. It's also where we keep the dog and cat food, which wouldn't be unusual at all . . . if we owned a cat or a dog.

We don't.

As we work, I try to think of a good way to mention Grandma Nora's visit. Something clever or witty or suave. I've got nothing. Especially not now that Mom thinks we came down here just to help her.

Thankfully, most of the cans are still lined up in their rows along the wall. Just enough have fallen that I know Dad was knocking them over on purpose. Not violently. That's *really* not his style. But if Dad was, say, digging out his suitcase from the closet or looking for a book from the shelves behind the cans, he could have easily—and passive-aggressively—knocked down this many.

"You know what this reminds me of?" Leslie says cheerfully as she restacks a section of soup cans. "In art class, Mrs. Garcia told us about a really famous painter who liked to paint cans."

"Yeah, right," I say, grouchy and tired.

"No, it's true," says Leslie. "I can't remember his name, but he painted all these pictures of cans like this one." She holds up a Campbell's chicken noodle can.

I snort. "That doesn't look much like art to me."

Mom's head pokes up from the other side of a wall of canned fruit. "Andy Warhol is one of the most recognized artists in the world. He was part of the pop art movement in the sixties."

"Yeah! That was his name," Leslie says. "Hey, Mom, did you ever paint any soup cans?"

Ever since I told Leslie that Mom used to paint, she likes to ask Mom about it. Leslie was too little to remember Mom's easel, and she hasn't caught on that Mom doesn't like to talk about it.

"No, I stuck with nature," says Mom. "Flowers and trees and things like that." As she says this, her head slowly disappears behind the canned fruit.

"Well, this is even better than a painting," says Leslie, flicking her hand at the stacks. "All that Andy guy did was paint cans. You have a whole sculpture."

"I forgot you had an art class last quarter." Mom's voice drifts from behind her wall of cans. "Did you like it?"

"I liked it so, so much. I wish we could just cancel P.E. or math forever, so I could do art with Mrs. Garcia all the time." Leslie chatters on about her art class, while I wonder how she has the energy to stay cheerful, even in the face of Grandma Nora and the coming apocalypse. I can't do it. So instead I give myself over to the task, and focus on the job in front of me. It's mindless work, repetitive and comforting. I take deep breaths.

I like the way Dad's den smells.

If I said that out loud, Rae and Melanie would probably tell me that I'm disgusting. There's a lot that I don't say out loud. There's probably a lot that they don't say out loud, too. Whatever the case, I think the best way to keep a friend is to keep most things to yourself.

Dad's books make the den smell musty, like old paper and mildew. On top of that, there's this nice metallic tang from the cans and, best of all, there's the smoky pipe smell. Dad doesn't smoke often, but in certain moods—usually when he's retreated most deeply into the land of denial—he jams the deerstalker on his head and brings out his pipe.

I think Dad likes the deerstalker because not only is it the hat Sherlock Holmes wears, but also it has earflaps. Built-in soundproofing. Dad will plop down in his chair, puffing away on his pipe with the earflaps tied so tightly that I worry he'll cut off his circulation. At these times, I'm positive Dad is pretending to be the brilliant Mr. Holmes, a man who can solve any problem. And you know what else? Sherlock was a bachelor.

I don't tell Dad that I love the pipe smell. I tell him it's the Scent of Death, because, let's face it, I *cannot* afford to lose my slightly more balanced parent to lung cancer or emphysema or some other equally horrendous disease that WebMD says is caused by smoking.

But right now it kind of feels like we've already lost Dad, and since he's probably boarding his plane, I take another guilt-free breath, enjoying the smoky scent. The pipe smell is stronger than usual. I bet he was smoking like a chimney last night when he decided to ditch us almost two weeks early. I hope Dad gets wedged in a middle seat on the plane. Between an obese old man and a lady with a screaming baby.

Don't think about Dad, I tell myself. Don't think about anything. Deep breath. Deep breath. Inhale. Grab a can. Exhale. Stack a can. Wipe the grit off my hands. Inhale—

I'm reaching for a can of creamed corn when Mom, who has left her spot behind the fruit barricade, walks by on the inhale. She reeks.

Well, that answers the Great Shower Question. No shower for Mom today. Or yesterday. And possibly not even the day before. She smells stale, like dirty laundry and sweat.

"You need a shower," I say, interrupting Leslie mid-description of her melted-wax "stained glass" project. The words pop out all on their own, and even I can hear how mean my tone sounds. Leslie, Mom, and I freeze.

Mayday. Mayday.

I'm not sure who is most horrified.

Leslie is still as a statue. She's clutching cream of mushroom soup in one hand and minestrone soup in the other. The minestrone slips from her hand and rolls across the floor.

This seems like the wrong time to mention Grandma Nora's visit.

Mom blinks furiously. I recognize the signs. We're in for it now. Her chest starts heaving. There will be tears and yelling. Then Mom will feel bad that she yelled, and she'll cry some more. This is what comes of slumber parties and Bambi eyes and getting sucked into the family drama. I'd rather be watching from the sidelines. Chad might have the right idea.

I should ask him to show me how to change the oil in our cars, so I can start spending more time in the garage.

"A shower is a great idea," Leslie says.

Is she trying to make things worse?

"I wish I'd thought of it first," she continues. "You do need a nice hot shower. You should take a break, and when you come down again, the den will be done. We're almost finished anyway."

The shoulders in the pink-pastel muumuu relax, and Mom's chest stops heaving. Her eyes quit blinking. She slowly nods. "That sounds . . . perfect. I do need to unwind."

I take back any mean thought I've ever had about my sweet, darling Leslie. Bambi is a diabolical genius.

Mom, or at least the woman who's supposed to be the parent around here, stops to pick up the soup, even though it's difficult for her with her bad knees. She gives the can to Leslie, patting her once on the head as she leaves the room. I notice that I don't get a pat on the head, but I'm too relieved that we've avoided a pink pastel meltdown to care.

Leslie and I go back to work. We can hear the stairs creak as Mom walks up to her room. When the creaking is distant enough, I turn to Leslie. "Thanks for the save."

Leslie shrugs. "I don't know if it really helped. We didn't tell Mom about Grandma Nora yet."

"You know what?" I say. "I've changed my mind. I'm not going to tell Mom anything."

55

Why should I? What will it change? We're all just sitting on the brink of a catastrophe, and there's nothing I can do about it. Sometimes I think the whole world is like that.

But I don't want to explain that to Leslie. She'll just want to swoop in and save the unsavable. So I say, "Grandma Nora and Mom are both adults. They'll figure it out."

"Are you sure that's a good idea?" Leslie bites her lip so hard that I wonder if she's going to cut herself.

"Right now, I have exactly one good idea," I tell her. "And it's called a nap."

Leslie studies my face. I'm not sure what she's looking for, but she must find it, because she turns her abused lower lip loose. "Okay, I'll do whatever you want. I trust you."

We go back to work.

When Mom finishes her shower, she'll probably rearrange everything Leslie and I are doing down here, but at least I won't trip over any more Bush's baked beans today. To pass the time, Leslie challenges me to see who can find the oldest can. It's a good distraction from worrying about Grandma Nora, and it makes the job a little more fun. Leslie wins. Her can of Del Monte sliced carrots is older than she is, and it's a full three years older than my can of French-cut green beans.

But by the time we're done, I feel like we've both won, because I've made a secret stash of cans—ones with bulging sides or missing labels. I couldn't risk doing it while Mom was working with us. She would have noticed. Leslie, on the other hand, is pretty much oblivious. So I hide the damaged cans under Dad's desk whenever Leslie's back is turned and, after she goes upstairs, I sneak them out to Chad's truck.

Chad and I keep a big black trash bag under his bench seat. We take turns filling it with stuff from around the house, and Chad dumps it whenever he's in town. We can't use the garbage can at our house, because Mom will dig stuff out of there. She's done it before.

But when we dump things in town, I don't think she notices. We're smart about how we do it. We only take little things, and only a few at a time. And we don't tell Leslie. She would confess everything the first time Mom looked at her funny. It's a good system, but it doesn't make much difference. It's like trying to save the Titanic by bailing water with a teaspoon.

Once the cans are in the truck, I stagger upstairs. I pause outside Chad's room. I never heard him come in from the garage, but he wasn't out there when I was hiding the cans. So I'm guessing he's in his room. I try to decide if I should warn him about Grandma Nora, but I don't hear any music or video games, so that means he's probably sleeping. Exactly what I want to be doing.

I decide not to bother knocking on his door. Instead I go to my room, where I throw myself on my bed. And in spite of everything—in spite of Dad leaving and Grandma Nora coming, in spite of Mom's red-rimmed eyes and Leslie's big, hopeful ones—I am dead to the world.

When I wake up, the sun is much lower in the sky, and the commotion I hear can only mean one thing: Grandma's here.

Dad likes his Shakespeare almost as much as he likes his Sherlock. Sometimes after he and Mom have had one of their battles and he has to face her again while he's still deep in his kingly persona, he'll say: "Unto the breach once more, dear friends, once more." Or something like that.

Anyway, when I hear the loud, semi-hysterical voices, I leap from my bed and charge into the breach. It's instinct. I don't think. I don't give myself time to wake up all the way. I just react. So the world feels like it's spinning and everything is a little fuzzy around the edges when I hit the bottom step.

I don't get a chance to look around before a pair of velvet-soft arms seizes me. Grandma Nora hugs me tight. Over her shoulder I see Mom, and Leslie is standing nervously behind her. Mom's face is blotchy and her eyes are wild. When we break apart, Grandma Nora's airplane-and-bubble-gum smell clings to me. I'll probably have to wash this shirt before I can wear it again.

"You look like you just woke up," Grandma Nora says. She reaches out to ruffle my bed head. One of Grandma Nora's many silver and gold rings catches on a tangle in my hair. She gives a little tug, and I barely stop myself from yelping out loud as Grandma Nora frees a few hairs from my scalp. The pain makes the world swim into sharper focus, and I get a good look at Grandma Nora for the first time.

"Hey, you cut your hair." I think back to the last picture I saw of her. She and Aunt Jill were on a scenic overlook. The beach behind them was overrun with elephant seals. Grandma Nora called them "amazing creatures"—she sent me an entire email about it. But I just thought they looked disgusting, like giant, bristly slugs (the seals, not Grandma Nora and Aunt Jill). In that photo, Grandma Nora's hair was soft and gray and poufy. Very grandmotherly. Now it's short and sassy, nary a gray hair in sight.

"And you dyed it," I add, wishing that my mom rather than my grandma would have been the one to discover hair coloring.

"Yes, I did," Grandma Nora says, patting her hair. "Thank you for noticing." She sends a stern look in my mom's direction. A mental scolding. It seems Mom hasn't yet commented on the new style. It's hardly fair to blame Mom for this; she looks like she's about to go into shock or pass out. "What do you think of it?" Grandma Nora asks me, still running her fingers through her hair, which is styled into these little reddish spikes all over her head.

The truth is: I don't like it. The top of her head looks like a cross between a troll doll and those little land mines on the computer game *Minesweeper*. It seems like something a teenage Goth-wannabe would try. I latch on to the teenage part of that thought train.

"It makes you look young," I say.

Grandma Nora beams. "That's just what the young man at the salon told me it would do. Well, we'll have plenty of time to finish catching up later. Now where would you like me to put my bags?" She motions to the suitcases that's right, plural—*suitcases* at her feet. "I want to get settled in before we start."

I went fishing with Dad once. Once was enough for both of us. I'm not sure who was more traumatized: me, Dad, or the fish. But right now Mom looks exactly like the one fish we did manage to catch. I remember how it flopped around out of the water, gasping for breath. Its frowny little mouth was opening and closing and opening and closing. Just like Mom's.

Grandma Nora shakes her head. "This is even worse than

I thought. Show me where to park my bags and we'll get started." She rubs her hands together.

Started? She hasn't sat down yet. She hasn't asked if Mom wants her help. This is going to be just as bad as I thought, maybe worse. And I was expecting Armageddon.

While I silently panic, my mother the codfish finds her voice. "I didn't know you were coming." Her voice is a few pitches higher than normal. "We're not really ready for company." Understatement of the year. "There's a bed-and-breakfast in town. Let me call and see if they have any rooms."

"You don't want me to stay with you?" Grandma Nora says, sounding too hurt to be believable.

"It's not that—" Mom says, wringing her hands like some tragic character in one of Dad's favorite Shakespeare plays.

"It's been *years* since I visited," Grandma Nora says. "I'll be so much more help if I stay here."

Which, of course, is exactly what Mom does not want.

Maybe if I'd been paying better attention, I would have predicted what happens next. I should have seen it coming. But I'm so involved in imagining different versions of the Balog Family Apocalypse that when Mom unwinds her hands and waves the white flag, her words catch me off guard. "If it's important to you . . ." Her voice fades away and she lifts her hands in a helpless gesture. ". . . I guess you'll have to stay in Annabelle's room."

Of course. Why didn't I prepare for this? It's worse than the apocalypse. Grandma Nora's stuff, spreading out and taking over my clean white spaces. There will be no place to live in my own house. How can I do my ritual if Grandma Nora's in there? I have to stop this. Have to, have to, have to. I try to think of a quick way to uninvite Grandma Nora, but I'm caught in a panic cycle and I'm too slow.

"Perfect!" says Grandma Nora. "And where will Annabelle sleep?"

No, no, no. Annabelle will sleep in her room. In her bed.

"Annabelle can sleep in my room," Leslie pipes up. I want to squash my sister, squash her like she's Jiminy Cricket.

"Wonderful!" says Grandma Nora, and she turns to face me. "Believe me. You do not want me for a roommate. Grandpa George used to say I snore like a grizzly. Well, that's all set." She's smiling, clearly thrilled to have so neatly evicted me from my own room. That done, she angles herself toward the top of the stairs and starts shouting for Chad. If her shouting is anything to go by, then I totally believe that she snores like a grizzly. She's deafening. "CHAD," she yells. "Where are you? Come down, dearest, and greet your grandmother."

There's no reply.

Grandma Nora turns to my mom. "Is he here?"

"I—I think so," Mom says, still looking bemused.

"Yeah, he's here," I say. It's about time he got dragged into the chaos.

"CHAD! CHAD! I know you're up there!" Between shouts, Grandma Nora starts addressing me, Mom, and Leslie. "Where is that boy? He needs to get his tushy down here and make himself useful. I'm not about to lug all this upstairs by myself. My hair may make me look twenty years younger, but that doesn't mean my back is any stronger—CHAD! CHAD!" She interrupts herself to yell some more. "WE KNOW YOU'RE UP THERE!" She turns back toward us. "And I have a fun idea. Once we get my bags upstairs, what do you girls say we go into town and grab some dinner? My treat. We can go over some of my ideas for how to fix up this place."

"Let's eat at Marcini's!" says Leslie, naming Dad's favorite restaurant. We tend to go there without Mom in times of trouble, and I can never decide if it's because Dad thinks of Italian food as comfort food or if it's because it makes Dad feel closer to Sherlock—he's forever telling us that there's a Marcini's mentioned at the end of his favorite Holmes novel.

Grandma Nora's eyes skirt around the room again. You never really get used to drowning in your own garbage, but it does kind of lose some of its shock value after a while. Really, it's amazing what people can get used to. So even though the house looks awful but normal to me, I can only imagine how bad it looks to Grandma Nora, and how much worse it would look to people from school. Grandma Nora opens her mouth as if she's about to continue her monologue, but Mom, who still seems to be experiencing symptoms of shock, suddenly speaks again.

"No!"

"Why shouldn't we go into town?" Grandma Nora asks her.

Panic flashes across Mom's face, and I wonder if she'll turn all blotchy and silent and fishlike again, but she doesn't. Instead, she stammers a bit and then spits out an excuse. It's totally lame and completely obvious that Mom is lying through her teeth.

"We—we—we can't plan to 'fix it up.' I don't want to—to— It's, um, we're having . . . I promised the kids a Family Game Night!"

It's a good thing we don't go camping anymore. If a grizzly wandered into our site, Mom would probably shove me into its open arms while she made her getaway.

It wasn't always like that. We used to have roaring fires and s'mores. I even remember Mom holding me on her lap while Dad told stories about Hamlet's father's ghost and Macbeth's murdered king. But things change. They get worse. And I try not to remember the better times. It only makes me upset. It's easier to accept the way things are if you don't remember the way they used to be.

"Family Game Night? Sounds great!" says Grandma Nora. She has the look of a tiger waiting to pounce, but for the moment, I guess Grandma Nora has decided to humor Mom.

Announcement: The apocalypse has been temporarily postponed.

"Let's order pizza," Grandma Nora says.

"Ooh, can we get pineapple on it?" Leslie asks. She hasn't stopped smiling since she volunteered to share her room with me. And now, with the mention of a Family Game Night, Leslie looks as if her wildest dreams have come true. Heaven help us all. She must think that Grandma Nora's visit is off to a great start.

"Fine," says Mom. "I'll take care of it." She shuffles off to the kitchen as fast as her bad knees will carry her.

I repress a sigh. I hate when we do this. It's not the first time Mom has tried these tactics. Maybe if we ignore the problem, it will go away. Maybe if we pretend to be a normal family, we'll become one. She always wants to put on the one-big-happy-family horse-and-pony show in front of other people. Sometimes it even seems like it's working. But the next day, our kitchen is still full of newspapers and Dad goes back to wearing a deerstalker cap and Mom still hasn't started painting again, and everyone is more miserable than they were before.

Grandma Nora shouts up the stairs some more. "Where is that brother of yours? CHAD! CHAD! CHAD!" She's so loud I am half-worried that she'll cause an avalanche. I can picture the hallway junk mail sliding down the stairs and burying us all under Valpak coupons and Pier 1 catalogues.

I shake my head to clear it—Leslie's File o' Death must be getting to me if I've started worrying about indoor avalanches. Or, maybe, it was seeing the newspapers clobber Leslie that got me worrying.

"CHAD, GET YOUR TEENAGE BUTT DOWN HERE. SO HELP ME IF I HAVE TO COME FIND YOU!"

Or so help Chad, I mentally correct her.

A door squeaks and Chad finally appears at the top of the stairs. He's rubbing his eyes, and his brown hair is sticking out in a hundred different directions. Actually, if his hair was red and just a little bit neater, he and Grandma Nora would have the same hairdo.

"Wh-who's making all the noise?" he asks. His voice is thick with sleep.

"I AM!" Grandma Nora booms. "Now will someone explain to me why everyone here thinks they can sleep till five in the afternoon on a Sunday? Did any of you even go to church this morning?"

Huh? What decade is Grandma Nora living in? Guess no one told her that we haven't gone to church in years and years. Not since the newspapers and Beanie Babies started piling up.

"What?" asks Chad, squinting down the stairs. He's leaning a bit to the left, his muscles tense like he's about to bolt.

"Grandma's here!" I try to sound happy, but I just sound fake. Sarcastic.

Grandma Nora notices. She stops yelling at Chad and twists her head around, like some sort of demented owl, to glare at me.

"And guess what? Guess what?" Leslie calls up to Chad. Grandma Nora doesn't glare at Leslie. There's no doubting that Leslie's excitement is genuine: She's bouncing on the balls of her feet and clapping her hands. She looks like a cheerleader. She probably will be one someday. There are times when I wonder how we're related. "Guess what, Chad? We're having a Family Game Night with Grandma Nora, and there's gonna be pineapple pizza and everything. Mom said so. Isn't that cool?"

Sure, Leslie. Sure. What could go wrong?

I retreat to the backyard. There's a wooden swing that hangs from the tree outside my bedroom window. Dad put it there, once upon a time when we were happy. It's the same cotton-wood that the plaid boxers got stuck in when I threw my room out the window.

I don't really have anywhere else to go, not with Grandma Nora moving into my room. And I can't hide in Leslie's room—I refuse to set foot in the Toy Catacombs a second before I have to.

As usual, I have my phone with me for company. I scroll through the texts from Rae, Melanie, Jenny, Amanda, and Drew, trying to distract myself from the thought of Grandma Nora cluttering up my room with foot creams and hand lotions.

When she followed Chad upstairs, I called out after her: "How long are you staying?"

"As long as it takes," Grandma Nora called back.

Not good.

"But when's your flight home?"

"Haven't bought the ticket yet."

Not good at all.

No wonder she brought more than one suitcase. I keep telling myself that Grandma Nora isn't Mom; Grandma Nora doesn't have any trouble throwing things out, but the anxiety continues to mount as I picture eyeglasses and heating pads and old magazines and woolen socks clogging up my space. There's someone in my room, touching my stuff, moving around my things.

Who knows what I'll be cleaning out of there once she leaves? If she ever leaves. Amanda's grandma "came for a visit" when we were in second grade, and she still hasn't left. And what if Mom sneaks things into my room while Grandma Nora's here? How can I check on it when Grandma Nora is living in it?

I trace patterns in the dirt under my swing with my foot. Circles and half circles. My phone buzzes, and when I check who's texting me, my heart gives a little pitter-patter. It's Drew.

Did you get your beauty rest after the party?

I can feel myself smiling. I text back:

What's your prob? Did you think I needed it?

I hit send before I realize that my answer might sound a little harsh. I was aiming for flirty. Rae tells me that sometimes when I'm trying to flirt I just sound mean. She can be pretty judgmental; still, she's right a lot of the time about stuff like that. But let's face it: If one bad text scares Drew off, then we're hopeless. My life (by which I mean my family) is not for the faint of heart.

I wait for his reply, twisting the swing in circles and then whirling around while the ropes unwind. I start going too fast, and my phone flies into the dirt just as it buzzes again. I scramble for it, relieved that no one is here to see what a dork I am. Drew has sent another text. I'm sitting in the dust, with the wooden swing bumping against the back of my head, but I'm happier than I've been all day. Drew didn't misread my text.

He's written back: "Yeah, you looked like an ogre. Better go to bed early tonite."

We go back and forth for a while. I call him a troll and a gargoyle. He calls me a harpy and a fossil. I guess he ran out of mythical creatures. He should probably pay better attention in school. Then my happy little bubble disappears.

Drew writes: "You live off Rainbow Rd, right? My cousin moved out that way. I'll stop by next time I visit him. Maybe Weds?"

No. Nonononononono. I have my Five-Mile-Radius Rule for a reason. It hasn't been easy, but the last time I had guests over was my tenth birthday, and I plan to keep it that way. I don't want anyone at school to know what our house is like. I don't want them to know that my mom is crazy. I'll get made fun of. Or, worse, people will feel sorry for me.

And then, worser and worser, there's always this quiet, niggling doubt in the back of my mind. We're talking Worst Case Scenario. I don't even like to think about it. But there's this little part of me that worries if the people at school found out, they wouldn't just judge me. They would try to help. Someone would call Child Protective Services. A teacher. Or a "friend." I've seen it on the news: kids who get put in foster care because their homes are too disgusting for them to live in anymore. I don't think our house is bad enough for CPS to take me and Leslie and Chad away, but I don't want to test that little theory. I don't want our family to split up.

So I try to think of a quick excuse, a reason to keep Drew away. I don't really want to lie to him, even though I have lied to people before about why they can't come over (everything from our septic tank exploded to there's a hantavirus outbreak).

But, for some reason, I want to be honest with Drew. Or, maybe, it's just that all my usual excuses are kind of gross. I mean, exploding septic tanks and rodent pee diseases are not the sort of things you want a cute boy to associate with you.

"Not the best time," I text. "My grandma's in town. She just got here."

"Cool!" he writes. "I'd love to meet her."

Suddenly Grandma's stuff cluttering up my bedroom doesn't seem so terrible. Everything is a little brighter. I'm feeling . . . optimistic. Leslie-like. It's a strange, unusual feeling. I notice how green the cottonwood and aspen leaves are and how yellow the dandelions in the grass seem. All because a cute boy said he wants to meet my grandma.

Don't get me wrong. I'm not about to let him come over. The Five-Mile-Radius Rule remains firmly in place, but a teenage boy does not ask to meet your grandma unless he likes you. I mean, I knew Drew liked me before, but now I know just how much.

And then, let's face it, because I'm no optimist, I'm no Leslie, and the universe doesn't want me to be happy for too long, catastrophe strikes.

"Time for Family Game Night," my mom shouts from the side door.

She's changed into her mint-green muumuu. Beware the pastels.

Family Game Night is a five-act Elizabethan tragedy. See, unlike Melanie and Rae and, apparently, Drew (we had a whole unit on allusion and creatures of mythology in literature), some of us hung on Ms. Leary's every word. I love English class. Actually, I love school. It's so neat and clean and calm and organized there. That's another secret. It doesn't help with the whole blending-in thing to like teachers or school too much.

But when everyone else was saying that class was boring, I was scribbling down Ms. Leary's every word about plots and pyramids and some guy named Freytag.

And now, Annabelle Balog presents...
The Tragedy of King Richard's Daughters

(I think that has a nice Shakespeare-ish ring to it, don't you?)

Dramatis Personae

GRANDMA NORA: meddlesome grandmother

MINT-GREEN-MUUMUU MOM: an emotionally fragile woman

CHAD: older brother

ANNABELLE: King Richard's elder daughter

LESLIE: King Richard's younger daughter

ACT I

SCENE: *The Balog family is seated around the death trap (a.k.a. their kitchen table), which is surrounded by still-wobbly stacks of newspaper. There are three mostly eaten pizzas in the center of the table. None of them have pineapple as a topping, but Leslie doesn't complain. There's a collection of empty glass jars—mostly old pickle jars—on top of the kitchen cupboards, a mountain of empty milk containers spills out of the pantry, and stacks of old egg cartons cover the counters.*

GRANDMA NORA (*with a deep, steadying breath*): So what games do you guys like?

75

LESLIE: Oh, anything.

ME: Do we even have any games?

Mom narrows her eyes at me.

LESLIE: We could play cards. I think there's a deck under the—

CHAD (*popping a last bite of crust into his mouth*): No can do. I've gotta go.

ME: What? Where're you going?

CHAD (*pushes back his chair, stands up*): Dinner with Sheila.

ME: But you just ate, like, six slices of pizza.

CHAD: That was an appetizer.

MOM: Sit down.

CHAD: Mom, seriously, Sheila and I do have plans.

GRANDMA NORA: Well, just send your girl a text and let her know that you'll be late. It can't take you long to play a game of cards with your aging grandmother. Who knows? The next time you see me, I might be in a coffin.

CHAD: Fine.

He sits and starts fiddling with his phone.

MOM: This isn't Family Card Night. It's Family Game Night. I'll be right back.

Mom shuffles out of the room.

GRANDMA NORA: I thought cards were a game.

ME: And I really don't think we own any games. Except maybe cards.

GRANDMA NORA (*shaking her head*): She's always been this way. When she gets an idea in her head, your mother has a hard time letting it go. I guess she wants us to play a board game.

CHAD: More like bored game. B-o-r-e-d game. Get it? (*He cracks up and goes back to his phone, probably texting his lame joke to Sheila.*)

LESLIE: I don't think they're boring.

ME: Depends on the game.

GRANDMA NORA (*staring in the direction of our pantry*): Where did all these milk jugs come from?

CHAD: The grocery store. (*He cracks up again.*)

ME: It also depends on who you're playing with.

GRANDMA NORA: And when is the last time anyone mopped the floor in here?

MOM (*shouting from the stairs*): I can hear you.

LESLIE: Well, our game night won't be boring.

ME: You can say that again.

ACT II

SCENE: *Mom returns a few minutes later, her arms full of battered old game boxes, which really shouldn't surprise anyone. This house has everything—Leslie once found a box of wigs in the closet under the stairs.*

ME (*as Mom reenters*): Where did those come from?

MOM: They were in Leslie's room.

LESLIE: They were?

ME: Do any of them even still have the pieces?

GRANDMA NORA (*still trying her best to get along with Mom*): I'm sure we'll find a way to make it work.

LESLIE (*leaning forward*): Which one are we gonna play?

CHAD: Why can't we just play cards? A couple of rounds of blackjack or something?

GRANDMA NORA: I don't hold with young people gambling.

MOM (*dumps the pile of games on the table and starts distributing them*): Let's see what we've got.

CHAD: We wouldn't have to play for money.

I sift through a beat-up version of the game Trouble. *It contains cards from* Sorry *and the buzzer from* Taboo. *I try the buzzer.*

It doesn't work. The batteries must be dead. Trouble has only one game piece.

ME: Well, we can't play this one.

MOM: I've got most of a backgammon set here.

CHAD: Actually, blackjack would probably be better if we didn't bet. It would take less time that way.

GRANDMA NORA: And I would wipe you out, young man. Know your opponent. First rule of cards.

ME: I'm pretty sure backgammon is a two-player game.

MOM: I know that.

CHAD (*standing up*): Perfect! You don't even need me here for that one.

LESLIE (*still rooting through the game Mom handed her*): Isn't *Monopoly* supposed to have money or something?

MOM: Sit down, Chad.

ME: I think *Monopoly* takes, like, three or four hours to play.

LESLIE: That sounds good.

CHAD (*sits back down. He waves his phone with the timer app on it.*): That's it. You're all officially on the clock.

GRANDMA NORA (*pointing toward Leslie*): Is that a hairbrush in your box?

LESLIE (*dangles an old wire hairbrush from two of her fingers. It's full of long black hairs. No one in our family has long black hair.*): Eww! Where do you think this came from?

CHAD: Here, let me take care of that for you.

He winks and snatches Monopoly, hairbrush and all, from Leslie. He flicks it away, and the box lands with a crunch in a nearby mound of grocery bags. A few loose bags scatter across the kitchen.

MOM: This game's good to go. It's even got (*she pauses to hold up a mess of papers*) the directions.

GRANDMA NORA (*with pursed lips*): How nice.

LESLIE: Oh goody, which game is it?

MOM: *The Game of Life.*

ACT III

SCENE: (*An aside—this is the part of the play that Ms. Leary called the climax—it's where everything changes.*) *We set up our board and discover that the Life money is missing. But we find the Monopoly cash in the Scrabble box. The wheel from Life is also missing, so Chad digs out the dice from Parcheesi.*

We find only four game pieces in the Life box. Grandma Nora volunteers to be a Scrabble tile instead of a Life car, but we can't find a single one of the pink and blue pegs that are supposed to drive the cars around the board. No one cares except for Leslie, who insists that we need them. She digs out a package of spaghetti and a couple of markers. The colored spaghetti people are closer to green and orange than blue and pink, but Leslie is satisfied.

LESLIE: Here's your noodle-man, Chad. Sorry the color is a little off.

CHAD (*without looking up from his phone*): No prob. Just stick in it my car.

GRANDMA NORA (*twitching her foot around under the table*): My foot keeps sticking to something under here.

LESLIE: Which car do you want to be, Chad?

ME: Give him the red one.

GRANDMA NORA: You know, your aunt Jill drives a red car. It's a convertible.

CHAD (*looks up at me, surprised*): Yeah, red's good.

GRANDMA NORA (*still twitching her foot*): Is there a sponge I can use? Or maybe I should just wipe this up with a paper towel? I think I saw some in the den.

MOM: Why were you in the den?

LESLIE: Here, Grandma Nora, why don't you be the banker?

MOM (*studying the directions*): Each player receives ten thousand dollars, so maybe each player can have one five-thousand-dollar bill and five of the one-thousand-dollar bills?

GRANDMA NORA (*takes the* Monopoly *money from Leslie*): I don't think there are thousand-dollar bills in *Monopoly*.

LESLIE: I can make some!

CHAD: No time.

GRANDMA NORA (*still twitching her foot every now and then*): How about we each just get two of the five-hundred-dollar bills and say they're worth five thousand each?

LESLIE: And we can pretend the hundred-dollar bills are one-thousand-dollar bills!

CHAD (*pockets his phone, leans forward, and rubs his hands together. He must have reached some kind of agreement with Sheila.*): Good enough for me. All righty, let's get this started. Youngest goes first?

GRANDMA NORA: That sounds good. Leslie, sweetie, you start.

MOM (*clinging to her directions, like they prove something*): No. These say, "All players spin the wheel. Highest spinner takes the first turn."

ME: But there's no wheel.

CHAD: I've got dice.

He rolls an eleven. No one beats his number, so Chad takes the first turn. Life gives players two options: business or college. The business route is shorter, and Chad sends his car that way.

MOM: Turn that car around. You will be going to college.

GRANDMA NORA: Oh, for heaven's sake, Pauline. It's just a board game.

MOM: Don't tell me how to raise my children.

ME (*muttering*): Cue the apocalypse.

LESLIE: What did you say, Annabelle?

CHAD: It's no big deal, Mom.

ME: Never mind, Leslie.

GRANDMA NORA: I never went to college, and I turned out just fine. (*She jerks her foot around. We can all hear the sticky sound from the floor under her chair.*) I certainly didn't need a college degree to keep my floors clean.

LESLIE (*quickly takes the dice from Chad*): I'm next. I'll go to college.

85

GRANDMA NORA: You know who else didn't go to college? Bill Gates. He didn't go to college, and he's the richest man in the world.

LESLIE: Oooh nooo! Study for exams. Miss next turn.

ME: Bill Gates went to college. He just didn't graduate.

CHAD: Ha! See, Les? That's why I didn't go. Now you lost your turn *and* you owe the bank forty thousand in loans.

GRANDMA NORA (*the sticky sound is coming from under her chair again*): Does anyone want to switch seats with me? This spot is giving me fits.

LESLIE (*shoving the dice at me*): Here, Annabelle. Your turn.

Chad's timer buzzes. He springs to his feet.

CHAD: You can have my seat, Grandma. It's been fun, but I'm already forty-five minutes late, so I'm outta here.

MOM: No, you're not.

CHAD: Yes, I am.

MOM (*stands up*): No, you're not.

LESLIE: Roll, Annabelle.

CHAD: Yes, I am.

Mom sits back down. She doesn't look at Chad.

MOM: Fine. If you don't want to be here, we don't need you.

Chad stomps out of the room. We hear his heavy footsteps on the stairs. I catch Leslie's eye and remember that it's supposed to be my turn. I roll. Grandma Nora takes her turn after me. Neither of us speaks, but we both take the college route. Mom is rolling the dice when Chad thuds back through the kitchen, smelling strongly of cologne. He slams the side door as he exits.

If this play was a Greek tragedy instead of an Elizabethan one, this is the part where the chorus would start wringing their hands and wailing. I feel like wringing my hands and wailing, too. But instead I just sit there and watch.

For the second time in three days, the whole house reverberates from Chad's door slam. I watch the newspapers in the "mid to upper 70s" column tremble and sway. Mom must have done a terrible job restacking them.

They shake. They swing. And they come crashing down.

Enter the rat.

There's a shocked silence. Followed by a squeak. The crashing newspapers must have startled the rat out into the open. We're all going to die from hantavirus. I want to strap a gas mask over my face. Surely we have one somewhere in this house. But I can't think where.

In the distance, a universe away from this rat-infested trench, Chad's truck roars to life. The sound breaks some sort of spell, and the remaining actors fly into action. Chairs scrape against the floor as Mom, Leslie, and Grandma Nora scramble after the rat. But not me. Now, I'm not proud of this. I'd like to think I'm one of those leap-into-action, once-more-unto-the-breach types. But I'm not.

Turns out, I'm the type who shrieks and jumps onto a chair.

Rat germs. Rat disease. Rat air particles. My gut reaction is to put as much space between me and the rodent microbes as possible.

Leslie, who by all rights should be the delicate flower up on a chair, is creeping toward the intruder. Mom is behind her, and Grandma Nora is just behind Mom. Grandma Nora has armed herself with one of the rolled-up newspapers, and as they close in on the rat, she suddenly pushes past Mom and Leslie.

"I'll get him!" she shouts, brandishing the newspaper like a Viking with a long sword.

"Don't hurt him!" says Leslie. She looks ready to save the rat by throwing herself on Grandma Nora's sword. If I know Leslie at all, she is totally planning to capture the rat, nurse it back to health, and free it in the woods behind our house.

At the same time, Mom grabs Grandma Nora by her sword arm but not out of any misguided concern for the rodent. No, her misguided concern is directed elsewhere.

"Don't rip my newspaper!" Mom shouts.

Meanwhile the rat, like my brother and my dad before him, has performed a vanishing act. The rat hightails it out of Family Game Night. Smart rat. His exit ushers us well into the fourth act.

See, the fourth and fifth acts of an Elizabethan tragedy are when things get really ugly. In act four, which Ms. Leary calls "the falling action," plans go awry. Everything comes undone. The poop hits the fan. And in act five, it all gets worse. Much, much worse. Act five is the part where everybody (and his brother) dies. Usually violently. They get stabbed or poisoned or buried alive or smothered with a pillow or baked into a pie.

The good news: No one actually dies in our little family tragedy. Still, what does happen is gruesome enough. With the rat's disappearance, Grandma Nora snaps back into tiger mode, and she chooses this moment to pounce.

"What. Is. Wrong. With. You," Grandma Nora shouts at Mom. She sounds so angry that each word is its own sentence. "You have a rat. In your *kitchen*. And you're worried about a newspaper?"

Mom doesn't answer. She drops to the ground and starts messing with the toppled newspapers.

"What are you doing?" Grandma Nora's eyes bug out so far I think they may pop.

When Mom doesn't answer, I chime in: "She's restacking the newspapers."

"Shut up, Annabelle," says Grandma Nora.

"Hey," Leslie protests softly, so softly that no one else hears. But I do. I send Leslie a small smile.

"What are you smirking at?" Grandma Nora asks me. I don't feel like explaining. I don't want to drag Leslie into this, so I just shrug. Grandma Nora turns back to Mom.

"What are you doing?" she repeats.

Silence.

"Answer me."

More silence.

"Answer me," Grandma Nora says yet again. She still wields the rolled-up newspaper, and when Mom continues to ignore her, Grandma Nora lifts her arm and thumps Mom with it. She whacks her squarely on the top of her head, like Mom is puppy who just piddled on the living room carpet.

See what I mean about things getting worse in act four?

And it keeps going downhill.

Mom drops her armful of newspapers and snatches at the rolled paper in Grandma Nora's fist. Grandma Nora doesn't let go. Leslie and I watch in shock and awe as Grandma Nora and Mom start a tug-of-war over the newspaper. They remind me of a couple of kindergarteners fighting over a favorite toy. As they wrestle—Mom yanking down and Grandma Nora pulling up—the paper unfurls, then rips. I can see a partial headline, which reads: FEELING THE PAIN. Beneath is a picture of football players in a messy heap on the ground.

Without warning, Grandma Nora suddenly drops her end of the paper, causing Mom and the football players to shoot backward. Since Mom never stood up, at least she didn't have far to fall.

"I can't believe this." Grandma Nora shakes her head so fast that her little red hair spikes flutter in the breeze. She's still standing, looking down on Mom, who is smoothing out the wrinkled football players. "The only real surprise," Grandma Nora continues, "is that Richard didn't leave you sooner."

Mom stops messing with her newspaper. Her voice is unexpectedly soft. "What?"

"You heard me. You're sick. This has to be an illness." Grandma Nora waves her hands in a sweeping gesture around our kitchen. "How could you keep this from me for so long? How could you do this to your family?"

"To my family?" Mom echoes Grandma Nora in the same soft voice as before.

"I've gotta go call Jill. This is so much worse than we thought." Grandma Nora spins around.

At her sister's name, Mom straightens up. Her voice is loud and harsh again. "Don't you dare call Jillian. This is none of her business."

"Yes, it is. She's your sister."

"Was my sister."

"She'll always be your sister, no matter how you feel about it."

"Huh. As far as I'm concerned, she's just some real estate agent. There's no reason for you to drag her into this."

"I disagree," Grandma Nora says over her shoulder. "After all, Jillian was a psychology minor. Or have you forgotten?" Grandma Nora says this with a great deal of dignity, as if she wasn't just fighting over a rolled-up newspaper like some sort of geriatric kindergartner.

Exit Grandma Nora.

Mom's not done shouting.

"Fine! Do what you want. But you should know Richard did NOT leave me. He goes to England EVERY YEAR." She slams around a few more newspapers. "EVERY YEAR!" Then when she realizes Grandma Nora isn't going to answer back, she creaks into a standing position and limps away.

Exit Mom.

End scene.

Leslie and I (and possibly the rat) are alone on stage for the final act. Leslie is standing there, looking like Bambi after his mother got shot. And I—I realize I'm still standing on my chair. I climb awkwardly down and try to lighten the mood. I scoop up the dice from the table and hold them out to Leslie. "Your turn."

"But I lost my turn. Remember?"

I can't help it. I laugh.

Leslie looks back toward the spot where the rat disappeared. Her shoulders start shaking, and at first I think she's laughing with me. It's all so over-the-top dramatic. Ridiculous, really. Then she makes a noise, and it's not a happy noise. I stop mid-laugh.

"Oh, Leslie," I say, and take a step toward her.

"It's not funny," she says, and she runs from the kitchen.

Exit Leslie.

But you can turn off bad feelings, and you can shove the hurt down so far and so deep that it fades. I box it up and picture lots and lots of duct tape holding the box closed. I put it out of my mind and focus on cleaning up *Life*.

I brush Leslie's homemade spaghetti people from the table into the trash, where they lie scattered over napkins and pizza crusts. I stand there and stare at them, the casualties of our Family Game Night, for a long time. They remind me of the dead bodies scattered across the stage at the end of *Hamlet*.

Then I shake myself out of it and shove the trash can back under the sink. Out of sight, out of mind. Once *The Game of Life* is all cleaned up, I rummage around under the sink where I hid our rat poison the last time this happened. Upstanding citizen that I am, I'm happy to do my part to stamp out hantavirus. I sprinkle the pellets behind some of the still-standing newspapers before re-hiding the poison. I don't want Leslie to find it. She can't even stand to swat a fly.

I wash my hands, tidy up a little more, and wash my hands again. I end up leaving the board games stacked in the center of our kitchen table. There's nowhere else to put them, and I'm not about to carry them back up to the Toy Catacombs. I don't think Leslie wants to see me right now. When the kitchen is as good as it's going to get, I meander down the hallway and pause at the foot of the stairs just outside the Forbidden Room. I really do wonder what Mom is keeping in there. Giant hair balls the size of tumbleweeds?

Eventually, I decide to camp in the linens room, formerly the living room. I shove a bunch of towels off the couch, stretch out, and turn on the TV, hoping it will keep my mind off the rat.

It's a little after eight o'clock and even with the sheets blocking most of our windows, I can tell it's still light outside. The sun hasn't quite set, but I drift off anyway after only fifteen minutes or so of watching the Tanner family dance around and sing about how happy, wonderful, great life is.

I hate *Full House*.

The TV is off when I wake early the next morning. I am snuggled under an afghan, and I wonder who turned off the television and got me a blanket. I like that it's an actual blanket, that whichever family member it was, they didn't just throw one of the holey towels or old sheets over me.

The little green lights on the cable box say that it's 5:45 a.m.

I dig down deeper under my blanket, wishing I could fall back asleep. You would think, if nothing else, that the sheets in the window seat would keep this room dark, but for the moment, it's disgustingly bright. Why is the universe cruel enough to give us time off when the sun comes up at this ungodly hour, and then send us off to school all winter when it's dark until practically noon?

I am lying on the sofa, trying to find the energy to plod upstairs—Leslie's room is really dark, as dark as the inside of a coffin, no matter the time of year—when quiet voices from the kitchen catch my attention. I recognize Grandma Nora and Mom. They don't sound angry, but I can't make out their words. I slide from the couch and inch toward the kitchen. I hesitate in the entryway with my blanket still wrapped around my shoulders. Mom and Grandma Nora are sitting at the table, steaming mugs in front of them. After last night, this is the last thing I expected to find.

"If it's any consolation," Grandma Nora is saying, "Jill told me that I handled you all wrong."

"I don't want to be handled at all," Mom answers, but her voice is quiet and sad rather than angry.

There's a silence, interrupted only by the clinking of cups and spoons. The smell of freshly brewed coffee fills the air, and I'm filled with a sudden desire to pour a cup and join them at the table where they're sitting and calmly sipping their coffee like normal adults.

As the silence stretches on, I give in to temptation and tiptoe over to the counter. I grab a mug and pour what's left of the coffee into my cup. Steam rises from the surface, and I inhale deeply before sidling over to the table. I feel their eyes on me, but Mom speaks as if I hadn't intruded.

"He hasn't answered any of my calls," she says, making my heart drop.

Dad. I didn't know she'd tried to call him.

Whenever Dad leads the UK tour, he always calls to let us know as soon as his plane has landed. Usually, he calls Mom once a day. Usually, he emails us a couple of times a week with updates on his trip, or pictures or facts he thinks we should care about, things like a picture of a wicker chair and a note that says, "Just thought you'd want to know that the Sherlock Holmes Museum has acquired the chair originally sketched by Sidney Paget in his drawing of Holmes." Leslie faithfully reads every letter of every note. I skim them. But it's still nice to know Dad hasn't forgotten us, that he's thinking of us—even if they're really boring thoughts.

Maybe his flight was delayed. Maybe he hasn't gotten to his hotel yet. Maybe he forgot to call because he's sleeping off his jet lag. I wait for Grandma Nora's reply, holding my breath because I'm scared she'll make things even worse by ripping into Mom again. But instead of yelling, Grandma Nora turns to me. "Annabelle, it's a lovely morning. Maybe you should take your drink out to the patio."

I can't believe she's trying to shoo me from the room. After their performance last night, I think I'm entitled to know what's going to happen next to this family. To my astonishment, Mom seems to agree with me.

"Annabelle's fine." Mom gives a halfhearted shrug. "She knows how it is."

"If you say so." Grandma Nora's every syllable drips with

doubt. I clutch my mug more tightly, inhaling the warm air and letting the heat melt into my hands. A few more quiet seconds tick by before Grandma Nora speaks again. "You said yourself Richard goes on this trip every year. I'm sure things will work out."

"I'm not," Mom says. Grandma Nora's eyes flick over to me again, and this time I wonder if she's right. Maybe I shouldn't be sitting here. Did my mom really just admit that things might not work out? She's never said anything like that before, at least not in front of me. And Mom's not done. "He wants me to clean the house while he's gone. He even gave me a list."

Another pause.

Then Grandma Nora says, "Have you thought about trying to follow his list?"

Mom gives a dry laugh. "I ripped it up."

More silence. More spoons clinking against coffee cups. I grip my mug so tightly I think I might burn my hands, but I can't seem to let go.

"He's done this before," says Mom. "But it felt different this time." Another unhappy laugh. It ends on something like a sob. "Oh God, I think he might really leave me. For the kids more than for himself."

And if he does, Leslie will blame herself.

Dad wouldn't just give up and let our family dissolve, would he?

Grandma Nora is right. I really shouldn't be here for this conversation.

"Then let's see what you can remember from that list, and start cleaning." Grandma Nora sounds more like herself this time: brisk, efficient, and ready to fix things.

At these words, my hands twitch around the mug. Something is different in the kitchen this morning. It feels like hope. But it's not the cotton-candy kind of hope. It's more desperate than that. It's a burning, scalding sensation. Afraid to even breathe, I wait for Mom's answer.

"Okay," she says.

Maybe Family Game Night wasn't such a tragedy after all.

I slip from my seat to rinse the coffee off my hands. Then I practically run from the kitchen. I want to dance and sing and shout the good news. For the first time—the first time ever—Mom has agreed to clean our house. But before I shout it from the rooftops, I want to tell Leslie.

"She's a little young for coffee, isn't she?" I hear Grandma Nora say as I scamper away. "It stunts growth, you know."

I don't stick around to hear Mom's reply. I dash upstairs and peek in Leslie's room. She is sound asleep, and she looks so peaceful that I decide to let her stay that way a little longer. Because as I stand there and survey the mounds of junk surrounding her bed, another equally pressing need occurs to me. This is an ideal time to take care of something I have to do. Have to, have to, have to.

I am so excited that Mom has actually agreed to clean up that I am almost careless while I perform my ritual. Grandma Nora's suitcases are on the floor, and some of her clutter covers my desk, but it doesn't bother me as much as it normally would. I walk the perimeter of my room, and I don't find a single piece of garbage tucked under the mattress or behind the desk. I grab some clean clothes from my dresser and hop into the shower, a smile on my face.

Once I'm dressed, I skip back down the hall to Leslie's room. I don't even braid or dry my hair. It's dripping trails down my back and seeping into my shirt. But for once I don't care. I cannot wait another minute to share my news. It feels like Christmas morning. No, it's better than that. I stopped liking Christmas when it turned into an excuse for Mom to add more stuff to her collections.

My stomach growls, but I ignore it and force myself to enter Leslie's room. Normally, I avoid this place as much as possible.

Poor Leslie. She was only four and a half when Mom started collecting seriously. For the first two-thirds or so of my life, I had pretty average parents. Chad had it even better. In elementary school we mostly had a mom who left the house. A mom who volunteered in our classrooms and taught Sunday school and cooked big family breakfasts on Saturday mornings. We had parents who read bedtime stories to us and tucked us in at night without having to swim through a sea of junk mail.

We had a family who ate popcorn and watched old Disney movies together on Friday nights, and Dad only occasionally tried to explain things like why *The Lion King* is really *Hamlet* in disguise or how *The Great Mouse Detective* is a tribute to Sherlock Holmes.

We had a family who ate off Mom's fine china on holidays and birthdays, a family who sat around the dining room table in the Forbidden Room. I really do wonder what she's hiding in there. Every tea bag my dad has ever used?

Whatever Mom is keeping in there, I doubt Leslie can even remember eating a single meal in the ex–dining room. She's had Mom and Dad at their worst for almost her entire life. Maybe that's why she's not bitter. She has nothing better to compare things with.

But, in spite of all that, today I find myself wondering: If things can go from good to bad, why can't they go from bad to good? I mean, if we used to be mostly happy, then why couldn't we be happy again? It's a scary thought; it's hard to hope. I don't want to be disappointed if I'm wrong, but right now I almost believe that we can get better.

Inside Leslie's room, it's not easy to hold on to my hopeful feeling. I'm always a little shocked when I realize that the Toy Catacombs are every bit as awful as I remember them. In my mind, I make a lot of things worse than they actually are. Not Leslie's room. I'm about to turn on the lights and start yelling my news, but I hear this little whimper and think that maybe she's having a nightmare. I read somewhere— probably on WebMD—that it's important to wake people gently if you're going to wake them from a bad dream.

So I creep inside the catacombs. I am halfway to the bed when I notice the demon teddy bear. It's watching me from the mountain of stuffed animals. Leslie's room is full of these massive piles, and the dark makes everything stranger, even more monstrous. The stuffed animals are a writhing mass of arms and legs and eyeballs. A sliver of light from the still-open door hits the white teddy bear, catching its red glass eyes. Who gives a stuffed bear red eyes?

The demon-possessed teddy bear with the glowing red eyes is just the right amount of freaky that I take a quick sidestep, trying to put as much distance as possible between me and the stuffed animals. I overstep and crash into a lar- gish mound of finger bones and ribs. I don't think there are any actual bones in the pile, but there might as well be. It's the Mound o' Building Toys—Lincoln Logs and Tinkertoys, K'NEX and wooden blocks—and it's just as sharp and loud as I imagine a stack of finger bones would be.

The sound of shifting plastic fills the room. Leslie whim- pers again, but she doesn't wake up. I scramble away from the Mound o' Building Toys. I'm nearly to her bed now. One more heap to go around and I'm there. I put as much space between me and Doll Mountain as I possibly can. The dolls are even creepier than the stuffed animals. No wonder Leslie has bad dreams.

Most of the dolls are naked. Their open eyes stare blindly into space like fresh corpses. Or zombies. Some of the dolls have vacant smiles. I can totally imagine them trying to eat my brains. Or rising from the bottom of a lake to exact revenge.

I am so busy trying not to run screaming from the dolls that I forget to check where I put my bare foot. I step on a piece of sharp plastic. Probably a piece from the Mound o' Building Toys. It hits the soft part of my arch.

"Ugh!" I grunt, and grab my foot. "Oww. Oww." I try a one-footed hop onto Leslie's bed. I miss and collide with the side of her mattress, which causes me to bounce backward and land in Doll Mountain. It's mostly squishy and rubbery. I should be grateful. It's a lot softer than the Mound o' Building Toys. But I'm not happy. The texture is too fleshy, too human-but-not. I start flailing around, trying to pull myself up out of this nightmare. I hear noises, and I'm not sure if they're coming from me or Leslie.

I shift positions and the dolls start raining down on me. I've been worried about a junk-mail avalanche, but now I know that I should have been worried about the dolls. I scramble to my feet.

Bam-bam-bam.

105

Things keep hitting me, and this time it's not the dolls.

"Aaagghh!" I scream, trying to whack away the missiles as they pelt me.

"Aaagghh!" Leslie screams.

She's awake. Good thing I didn't just turn on the lights or yell from the doorway. This has turned out so much better. So gentle and calm.

Bam-bam-bam. I'm hit again.

"Ouch! Stop it! Ouch!" I say. Leslie is standing on her bed. Bunbun, her stuffed rabbit, is lying at her feet, along with an array of ammunition: blocks, Matchbox cars, and small plastic toys, the kind that look like they came from a Happy Meal. Her arm is back as if she's about to release another volley. I'm starting to think Bambi has more backbone than I gave her credit for.

"It's me! It's me!" I say.

Leslie blinks. She shakes her head.

"Annabelle?"

"Yeah," I say. "Who'd you think it was?"

She drops her ammo. "I dunno. I guess I thought you were part of my dream." She bends down to turn on her bedside lamp. I limp to the bed and sit. "Why are you up here?" she asks.

"We're sharing a room while Grandma Nora's visiting. Remember?"

"Yeah." She sits beside me. "But you didn't come up last night."

"I know. I didn't think you'd want me around."

"I always want you around." She reaches over and hugs me. I squirm, but Leslie tightens her hold. "Will you sleep up here tonight?"

I nod. Then I remember the reason I came up in the first place. "Leslie, you'll never guess—"

The overhead light flicks on, interrupting my news. Grandma Nora and Chad are standing in the doorway.

"What's going on up here?" Grandma Nora asks. She looks concerned. "I could hear you both screaming bloody murder, even over the racket in the kitchen."

"Yeah," says Chad. He's in his boxers, and he doesn't look concerned at all, just tired and annoyed. "Some of us are trying to sleep."

"Sorry," says Leslie. "Annabelle startled me is all. It was an accident."

"Whatever. Just keep it down." Chad scrubs a hand through his hair, and he stumbles back toward his room.

Grandma Nora gives us another worried look. "Annabelle, I really think you might be too excitable for coffee. And, Leslie, is that a frying pan in your bed?"

I twist around. Half of Leslie's queen-size is full of artillery. And it's not just Matchbox cars and Happy Meal toys.

There's also a frying pan, a baseball bat, and—is that a hammer?

We hear Chad's door close, and Grandma Nora's entire body stiffens. She reminds me of a hunting dog. Underage coffee consumption and bedside frying pans forgotten, she turns and stalks toward my brother's room. "Where do you think you're going?" she calls after him. "It's almost seven in the morning. There's no need for you to go back to bed. Up and at 'em, boy. Why, when I was your age, I was already waiting tables. It's time you—"

I cross the room and close Leslie's door.

"No more weapons in your bed," I tell her.

"But it makes me feel safe."

Guilt, guilt, guilt. I've been so busy worrying about my room that I didn't notice my little sister feels like she has to go to bed *armed*. "Well, it's dangerous," I say, pointing at the hammer. "You could really hurt yourself."

Leslie is fidgeting with her nightgown. "I really only sleep on half of my bed."

"Right," I say. "But while Grandma Nora's here, I'm going to sleep on the other half. And—" I pause dramatically until Leslie stops playing with the fabric of her nightgown and looks at me. "And when Grandma Nora leaves, you won't need it anymore."

"Why? Are you moving in with me for always?"

"Even better," I say.

"I'm moving into your room?"

"No," I say. "Even better."

"What?"

Rather than answering, I walk to the stuffed animals and pluck demon teddy bear from the pile. Then I dig around in Doll Mountain, searching for the creepiest one I can find. It takes me a minute before I settle on an eyeless doll with Xs over her mouth.

Leslie is at my elbow. "What are you doing?" she asks again and again.

I pull the dusty curtain out of the way and pry her window open.

"Leslie," I say as I straighten up. I can feel my lips stretched into a huge smile. "It's a brand-new day, and we're cleaning up."

"No!" says Leslie. "We can't. You were there last night. Mom will be so, so mad."

I shake my head. "Mom told Grandma Nora that she wants to clean the house."

"Really?"

I nod. I want to believe that things can change for the better, but I don't think I'll believe it until I see it. So just in case Mom's bout of sanity is short-lived, I add: "Really. They're going to work downstairs, and I think we should make it a surprise that we're starting on the upstairs."

"A surprise?" She sounds doubtful.

"Dad will love it. He told Mom to clean out the house while he was gone."

"Well, I guess that's true," says Leslie. "Did Mom really say she wants to clean up?"

"She really did." I'm smiling again.

This time Leslie smiles back.

"Okay," she says.

I hand her Creepy Doll. I'm still holding Demon Bear. "On three," I say. "One, two—" I pull my right arm back, ready to fling it forward with all my strength. When I say "three," Creepy Doll and Demon Bear soar in graceful arcs, landing in a dirt patch near the garage.

The kitchen is a disaster when Leslie and I come down for breakfast. I haven't even been upstairs all that long, maybe a half hour or forty-five minutes . . . I mean, no one ever accused Grandma Nora of being slow. But still. This is ridiculous. She's like a hurricane.

In the short time since Mom agreed to clean, half the pickle jars have been taken down from on top of the cupboards and are scattered everywhere. The egg cartons have been taken down from the counters and are all over the floor. Every single drawer and cupboard is wide-open. One drawer, the Drawer o' Sharp Things, has been pulled completely off its track and is dumped out—in the dishwasher of all places.

The breakfast nook isn't any better. Mom has dismantled

several of the newspaper towers, and they're spread across the room: over the table, the chairs, the floor . . . Hurricane Nora, meanwhile, is storming through the pantry, emptying it of every milk carton in sight. Leslie and I watch the containers as they fly from the pantry, one after the other, in a series of perfect parabolas before crashing in a haphazard heap in the middle of our kitchen.

Chad is nowhere to be seen. I wonder if he went back to sleep or if Grandma Nora successfully bullied him into doing something. Grandma Nora is whistling, so maybe she won her little showdown with her grandson.

Or maybe she's just in a good mood because she feels like she's fixing something. She and Mom aren't talking, but they seem to be getting along—working side by side like this. I can't help but wonder how long it will last.

"Good morning!" Leslie says, recovering more quickly than I do. She's in her nightgown and there's sleep goo in her eyes, but she's smiling like we've just won a billion-dollar lottery. She must have mistaken the dismantling of our kitchen for progress. But I know better. Nothing has been taken outside or thrown away yet. Rearranging the mess does not a cleanup make. I'm not sure Grandma Nora knows what she's doing.

Mom is crawling around her newspaper forest. She barely looks up at Leslie's greeting. She is so focused on her job that she just grunts a short "Morning" and keeps rearranging. I wonder if the papers are still ordered by their weather reports, or if she's working on a new system. I guarantee that—even on the off chance she is actually planning to throw them away—there will be an order to how she does it.

Unlike Mom, Grandma Nora stops working. She sticks her head out of the pantry. "Good morning, Sunshine," she says, chucking a last milk gallon into her heap and wading toward us through the knee-deep mess.

I stare at the milk cartons. They are way grosser than I ever realized. We've been living in a house with a closet full of *this*? I haven't given the milk containers much thought before. They're normally just one more piece of the clutter to ignore. If your brain couldn't tune out background details like crusty milk jugs, then people's heads would explode the instant they walked inside our house. Not that we let people inside our house.

But when the milk gallons are in a giant heap in the center of the kitchen, they're kind of hard to ignore. Mom usually rinses the gallons out before cramming them in the pantry (odd-numbered expiration dates on the right side, even-numbered expiration dates on the left) but some gallons weren't rinsed well. They're caked with thick yellow crusts. Others are worse. They have grayish-green lumps growing up the sides. Half the jugs are bulging with built-up pressure; they look ready to burst. And it could be in my head, but this morning, I swear our kitchen smells like spoiled milk.

It's moments like these that remind me why the Five-Mile Radius is so important. It's bad enough that my grandmother has seen this, but if a non–family member ever got a peek at this dump, I think I would literally—and I am not exaggerating—die of embarrassment. And if death by mortification isn't a thing on WebMD, then I guess it'll become one. I'll be the first.

I've never even met one of Chad's girlfriends. He hasn't ever brought one home. It's a good choice. If Grandma Nora doesn't get this cleaned out, we're all doomed to be alone. None of us will ever have a serious boyfriend or girlfriend or get married. Or, maybe, I'll just tell my husband that my parents live in Timbuktu.

Grandma Nora plants a kiss on Leslie's forehead, and then squeezes me in a quick little side hug. Meanwhile, Mom continues crawling among her newspapers. She always did tend to block everything and everyone else out when she gets super focused on a project. It won't last. Something, probably leg pain, will distract her before too long. Prediction: She'll be camped out on the couch with an ice pack on her knee by noon.

"What's, uh, what's going on?" I ask. This is my diplomatic way of saying that while I know they're cleaning up, it doesn't look like much of a cleanup.

Mom ignores me. She fans through a pile of newspapers on Dad's chair.

Grandma Nora answers: "You know perfectly well what's

going on. You were there when we decided. But, Leslie, you'll be glad to hear that your mother and I have agreed to fix up some of the mess around here."

I can't seem to stop myself from saying: "This is fixing up the mess?" I've seen news footage of national disasters that looked better than this.

"If you can't pitch in with a good attitude, then just turn that little tushy right around and get back upstairs." Grandma Nora twirls her pointer finger in a few tight circles.

"But Annabelle is pitching in." Leslie comes to my rescue. "She's going to help me cl—"

I give her a soft kick in the shin and small shake of my head.

"Oh, right," says Leslie. "It's a surprise."

Mom doesn't notice. She's muttering something about "precipitation levels." Grandma Nora, though, softens her expression. I don't care if she knows what we're up to, just so long as she doesn't clue Mom in too soon.

"Anyway," I say, "Leslie and I are going to grab some breakfast."

Grandma Nora looks around the kitchen as if she's just now realizing what a mess they've made. With a rueful nod, she says, "Okay, but you better eat in the other room." Leslie and I have a little trouble locating clean bowls and spoons, and digging out the milk and cereal, but eventually we get everything together and settle in the linens room.

When I was younger and there were still rules, it was a hard and fast one that we couldn't eat on the couch, and for some reason that always stuck with me. The rules you learn when you're little have a habit of doing that. So Leslie and I swaddle ourselves on the floor in a pile of old quilts next to the blocked-off window seat.

"All right," I say, leaning forward to look Leslie in the eyes. "How're we going to do this?"

"What do you mean?" she asks.

"How do you want the cleanup to go?"

"You want to make a plan?" she asks between large mouthfuls of Cap'n Crunch. "Why? Can't we just start?"

"You saw the kitchen, didn't you?"

"Oh," says Leslie. She swallows. "I guess you're right. Wait a second, okay?" Leslie sets her bowl on the wood floor, and I watch the pink bottoms of her feet disappear around the corner. A minute later, she returns with her markers and a notepad. Leslie resettles herself in the quilts and opens the pad to the first page. She writes "Leslie and Annabelle's Cleanup Plan" at the top of the page. It takes her forever because she alternates between the pink and yellow markers for every letter and draws a lot of lopsided hearts around our names. Her face gets this serene look while she draws. For a while, I just let her decorate the page as I eat. Her expression reminds me of the way Mom used to look when she held a paintbrush.

Leslie's Cap'n Crunch slowly turns into giant soggy squares. I'm on my third bowl before I finally stop her.

"It's good enough," I say when she pulls out the blue marker and is about to start adding clouds between the hearts.

"Oh, sorry." She recaps the blue marker.

"It's fine if you want to take notes." I actually really like the idea of someone writing down everything I say. "Let's just get started."

Grandma Nora's raised voice interrupts us. "Be reasonable," she's saying.

"Okay," Leslie says, a little louder than necessary. She pulls out the purple marker and writes: "Step #1."

"Don't be sentimental." Grandma Nora's voice booms.

I don't hear Mom's reply. I don't want to. Instead, I start outlining my ideas for Project Catacomb Extraction. I talk just loudly enough and just fast enough that Leslie and I both have to concentrate on what I'm saying rather than on the squawks coming from the kitchen.

We won't try to do everything at once, like Mom and Grandma Nora are doing in the kitchen. We'll sort through each pile, one at a time, and we'll divide each big pile into three smaller ones: garbage, giveaway, and keep. I'm going to make sure that the keep pile is tiny. Minuscule. Infinitesimal. We'll put the garbage in black bags, and I'll get Chad to drive it into town. There's a Dumpster behind the high school where we take Mom's stuff whenever we manage to smuggle a load out, and there's a Goodwill in Chatham. The giveaway pile can go there. And whatever doesn't fit in Leslie's closet when we're done, well, I'll just send it out the window.

"Get it?" I ask. "No nonessentials. You can only keep what you have room for. If it doesn't fit, it has to go." Like Mom, Leslie can get sentimental over things. She has a shoe box full of old movie-ticket stubs and programs from school plays, and birthday cards. If it fits in the closet, she can have it. Otherwise . . .

Leslie stops writing. She nods, looking very serious.

By the time we're done, Leslie's cereal is way past soggy. She may have to skip the rest of her breakfast anyway, because the voices from the kitchen are getting harder and harder to ignore.

"You can't be serious!"

"It's my house. Just let me do it my way."

"But there are dozens of milk jugs here. It'll take forever."

Mom mumbles something. I can't quite make out her words.

Grandma Nora is in grizzly mode, though, and I can hear her clear as a bell: "Expiration dates? Why? The gallons are empty. Gone. Finished. Who cares when they expired?"

Mom's reply is still fuzzy, but I swear I hear the words *special dates.*

"We're not saving any of them!"

I hear the clunking of dozens of milk jugs being shuffled around. Mom better watch out if Grandma Nora is in arm's reach of a newspaper. More clunking. More raised voices.

The morning's fragile truce is officially over.

"Let's go upstairs," I tell Leslie.

She nods, and we scamper away, leaving the remnants of our breakfast on the ground next to the pile of quilts. I hope Grandma Nora finds it before it gets too warm. The last thing we need around here is more spoiled milk. We'll have to risk it, though, because I'm not about to go back in that kitchen. Not even for the winning ticket in a billion-dollar lottery.

The cleanup gets off to a smooth start. For me and Leslie anyway. We begin by sorting through Doll Mountain, and the catacombs start slowly, oh so slowly, to transform. I am half-hopeful that after years and years of living in a toy sepulcher, Leslie will have a normal bedroom by the end of the week. But it's only a half hope at best, because downstairs World War III is in full swing. And that sort of thing tends to put a damper on your outlook.

I wish I could say that Mom and Grandma Nora were waging their war on the house, but they're too busy fighting each other. I'm not really sure who's winning. Most of the time it sounds like they're both losing. Like we're all losing.

We've barely seen Chad. It's not unusual for him to

disappear when things get rough. He's almost as good at the Disappearing Act as Dad. But while Dad most often disappears under the flaps of his deerstalker, Chad is usually off with his friends. He's super popular.

I've only got, like, three real friends. Plus Amanda, I guess. She's always around. We're just not as close as we used to be. I don't even know who she has a crush on. Amanda and I didn't have a big fight or anything. We just kind of drifted apart after Rae moved to Colorado. Last year, I barely even saw Amanda at school. Someone, I think it might have been Jenny, told me she thought Amanda was reading in the library at lunch most days. Then, this year, Amanda asked if she could eat lunch with us, and now I think we might be learning how to be friends again.

And, of course, there's Drew. He would make a fifth friend. But, again, I'm not really sure if he counts.

Either way, it's hard to keep friends when half your life is this huge secret and you can't let them within five miles of your house. I can't wait until I can drive, like Chad. He doesn't have to wait for school to see his friends.

I bet Chad couldn't even count all his friends. He's always hanging with "the guys" or going out with some girl or at a party or sleeping on the futon in Will Williamson's basement. Will is probably Chad's version of Rae. Like me and Rae, Will and Chad have been best friends since the start of middle school. And from what Chad says, Will has a great house. His family has a backyard basketball court. Sometimes it seems like Chad lives with the Williamsons. Once I even heard Will's mom make a joke about it, calling Chad her "adopted" son. Chad cracked up. I didn't think it was funny.

It's not like I blame Chad for avoiding home. Well, I might as well be honest. I do blame him. I blame him a lot. But I understand why he does it: His room is almost as bad as Leslie's. Mom divided it into quadrants: one-fourth old exercise equipment, one-fourth used camping gear, and one-fourth unused paint cans. And I don't mean her watercolors. I think she actually threw those out.

Near the start of her collecting phase, Mom stopped painting on watercolor paper and started stockpiling paint cans. For a while there, she really had this thing for house paint. She was always bringing it home or having it shipped to the house—mostly in dozens of shades of baby blue, light pink, pastel yellows, and spring greens. It's been a long time since she brought home new paint, though . . . as far as I know.

The smallest fourth of Chad's room (hey, I never said all quadrants were equal) is the little corner with his bed, music system, and desk. There's also usually a pile of clothes on the floor next to his bed. I don't think Chad has used his closet in years. It's behind a stack of mostly broken camping chairs.

As Leslie and I work on her room, I keep thinking that, maybe, we can help Chad do something about his room once we're done with hers. Maybe he won't want to spend so many nights in the Williamson's basement if he's got a tent-free, exercise bike–less room.

I've never offered to help Chad before. I don't know why. I've asked Leslie about a hundred times, but I just watched Chad's room get worse and worse. It never occurred to me that I could help him. I guess I always assumed that since he's four and half years older than me, he could figure it out for himself. I mean, I cleaned up my room when I was only ten.

I bump into Chad in the upstairs hall on Monday night, just as Leslie and I are wrapping up Day One of the Catacombs Extraction.

"I haven't seen you all day," I say. "Where've you been?"

"At work," he says like it's obvious. As if I should have known, when he never even told us he was applying places.

"You got a job?"

"Yeah. How do you think I got Grandma Nora off my back this morning?"

"Did you go get a job just so she'd leave you alone?" Just so he has an excuse to get out of the house while she's visiting?

"No, I had one lined up before she came. I've gotta pay for gas somehow."

"Where are you working?"

"The Exploding Hoagie." He skirts around me and starts walking down the hall.

"Wow!" I say, following him. "That's so cool."

And I really mean it. I'm not being sarcastic. I've always been a little obsessed with The Exploding Hoagie. For a fast-food kind of place, it's really clean. It's not one of those tacky, overdecorated restaurants. If I wanted to eat surrounded by clutter, I could just stay home. And it always smells like fresh bread. But my favorite thing about The Exploding Hoagie is the meat slicer. I love watching the employees use the meat slicer. There's something mesmerizing about it: the low hum of the machine, the smooth back-and-forth motions, the giant hunks of ham being shaved into razor-thin pieces.

I'm still trailing behind Chad when he starts to shut the bathroom door.

"Hey," I say, sticking my foot in the doorway before he can close it. This is the first time I've really talked to him since Family Game Night, and who knows when I'll catch him again? "It's been pretty crazy around here. With Grandma Nora and all."

He gives a dry chuckle. "I can only imagine."

I roll my eyes. Chad could do more than imagine if he would stick around for longer than an hour or two. I take a step back and try a different approach. "Have you heard from Dad yet? Like, do you know if his plane landed?"

A dark, uncharacteristic look crosses his face.

"No."

"Are you worried about him?" I ask.

"I would be if I didn't think he was ignoring us on purpose."

"What?" I haven't quite thought of that yet. It's a little like being slapped.

"He's just getting even with Mom," Chad says, and he shuts the door in my face.

I'm not done talking to him, though. There's so much more I want to say. But I can't quite find the words, so I end up asking the door: "Do they let you use the meat slicer at work?"

It doesn't answer.

Neither does Chad. I'm sure he can hear me. I can hear him. But the only response I get is the sound of the toilet flushing. Then the shower starts, and I stand there, trying to decide if I should wait until Chad comes back out. Maybe if I ambush him, I can blurt out the things I really want to say: things about Dad and Mom and Grandma Nora and the fighting and Leslie's nightmares and divorce and custody and CPS.

Or, if I can't manage that, I can at least ask if Chad will take me to The Exploding Hoagie with him tomorrow. Leslie could come, too. I've got enough money to buy us chips and fountain drinks for his entire shift. Or Leslie and I could hang out at the park or the library. If the rest of Grandma Nora's visit is going to be as loud and awful as it was today, I'll do anything to get out of the house for an afternoon or two.

I never get the chance to ambush Chad. The sound of creaking steps sends me running for cover. I don't know if it's Grandma Nora or Mom on the stairs, but unless you want to get drafted, it's best to hide from grown-ups on the warpath.

Later that night, after Leslie and I are both ready for bed, I stand on her mattress and survey our progress. We're pretty much finished with Doll Mountain. It was one of the biggest piles in Leslie's room, so even though there are still piles and piles to go, I feel like we've accomplished a lot.

While I stand on the bed—which is no longer doubling as an armory—Leslie is standing near the trash bags of discarded dolls, the ones with no eyes or missing limbs or shaved heads. She plucks one from the bag. It has no arms.

"Put it back," I say.

She looks at me a little guiltily. "But they seem so sad." Leslie fingers the empty sockets where the arms used to be. "I don't think they want us to throw them away."

When I look at those dolls I have to try not to think of Chucky, a horrible doll-murderer from yet another terrifying movie Rae forced me to watch at one of our sleepovers. But when Leslie looks at them, I'm sure she's thinking of *Toy Story*. She used to watch it almost as often as she watched the princess movies . . . before Mom boxed up the DVDs and we stopped our Friday Disney nights.

"Stop feeling sorry for it," I say. "It doesn't have feelings. It's not alive."

"I know," says Leslie. She puts the armless doll back in the bag, but she does it with a sigh.

Tuesday morning, we decide to conquer the stuffed-animal pile. It's slightly less traumatic than Doll Mountain, but it takes twice as long. For one, there are more stuffed animals than dolls. Plus, it's harder to decide which stuffed animals should be thrown out and which ones are okay for Goodwill.

Our progress is interrupted shortly before lunch, when I reach into the pile and feel something crunchy. I hold it up before realizing that it's a stuffed dolphin caked in ancient throw up. I shriek and toss it across the room. All I want is to get Pukey as far away from me as possible. I don't hit Leslie with it on purpose.

"Ew! What was that?" she says.

"A dolphin."

"Why is it crunchy?" Leslie looks at it lying on the floor at her feet. She doesn't bend down to touch it.

"I think it's covered in old vomit," I say. "I have to go wash my hands."

I'm almost out the door when something nails me in the back of the head.

"Hey! What was that for?"

Leslie shrugs, a little smile pulling at the corners of her mouth. "You started it."

"And I'll finish it," I say, grabbing a one-eyed panda and a ladybug Pillow Pet.

By the time Leslie calls for a truce, I realize that we've undone half our morning's work. But at least our war is fun. Based on the noises from the kitchen, Mom and Grandma Nora and World War III remain in a stalemate.

It's long after we would usually eat lunch when Leslie offers: "Paper-Rock-Scissors?" which is how we've been deciding who has to go downstairs whenever we need something.

"Nah," I say, examining my chapped hands. I have to leave at least three or four times an hour to wash my hands, and I've practically washed the skin off them. "I'll go down. I want to find some gloves. Do you want a pair, too?"

She shakes her head no.

"Are you sure?" I ask, concerned that she hasn't washed her hands once today. It seems like a recipe for salmonella, hantavirus, or the plague.

"Yeah, I'm sure," Leslie says. "This is my room. I live in here. It just doesn't feel that dirty to me."

It should. Guilt, guilt, guilt. Jiminy is chirping up a storm right now. It's like Leslie doesn't know what it means to have a clean room. She's so used to the filth that she doesn't even see it. I walk downstairs, imagining two hands pushing away the guilt—pushing it out the door, out the window, out of the state, off the map. Squashing the cricket. I'm so distracted that I'm in the downstairs hall before I realize that something is wrong. Terribly wrong.

It's quiet. World War III has raged for the last two days, and now there is only silence. But it's not a peaceful quiet. It's a dead quiet. Quiet like a battlefield when only the corpses are left.

I search for the source of the silence. Since yesterday morning, the house has been filled with noise: Mom's collections being schlepped around, doors slamming as Grandma Nora takes things outside and doors slamming again as Mom brings it all back in, accusations hurled as Grandma Nora calls Mom a liar for saying that she wanted to clean up and counteraccusations as Mom insists that she does want to clean but Grandma Nora is ignoring her wishes and belittling her feelings. That's usually when the past gets brought up and things are said that I don't understand, that I don't really want to understand.

There's been shouting and screaming, and the phone has been ringing off the hook. Mom keeps answering, even though it's always Aunt Jill, and Mom has refused to speak to her sister for years. I think she's hoping that it will be Dad. I also think Mom kind of enjoys hanging up on her sister. I hope Leslie and I are never like that.

Dad still hasn't called.

I've decided Chad is probably right. When Dad left, he was upset enough that he went into hiding from all of us, not just Mom. It's not fair. He should at least send an email to let his kids know he didn't die in a fiery crash over the Atlantic. He didn't. I checked the news—no recent plane crashes. So, unless he's been kidnapped by some modern-day Moriarty, I'm assuming he's alive and well. I could email Dad first. I could check in with him, instead of waiting for him to check in with us. But I don't really want to do that . . . because what if he doesn't write back?

The only sound that interrupts this afternoon's silence is the distant hum of an airplane. I'm surprised I can hear it all the way in the house, but then I notice that the front door is cracked open. I'm about to close it when I hear Mom and Grandma. I peek outside and see that they are seated on the top step of the front porch. Mom is leaning against Grandma Nora, and Grandma Nora is rubbing her back in a circular pattern.

No corpses yet. I count this as a victory.

"Please consider it," Grandma Nora is saying. "Jill thinks that it would really help you to start painting again. It would be like therapy."

This sounds just interesting enough that lunch can wait a bit longer. I crouch down, careful to stay concealed by the door. Their backs are to me anyway.

"Stop it, just stop it," Mom says. She wipes her face with her hands and pushes away from Grandma Nora, who drops her hand from Mom's back. "I can't believe that you and Jill of all people would have the nerve to tell me I should—" She takes a deep breath. "That you would say I should try painting as therapy. You know I hate it when you talk to Jill about me."

"I'm not going to apologize for talking to my own daughter. Whatever your differences with your sister are—"

"You know what my differences with Jill are."

"I refuse to speak with you about George's will one more time."

"It's about a lot more than the money, and you know it."

"Jill needed an MBA. If she wanted to get any further."

"What about art school? What about what I wanted?"

"We've been over this a million times. George left it up to me."

"That's only part of it," Mom says with a little hiccuping voice. "Even before—before he died, you've always done this, acted like I don't matter. Like what I wanted didn't matter, because I'm not perfect like she is. You make me feel so broken."

I think Grandma Nora will deny it. I don't expect her to admit that she meddles. She's supposed to deny that she thinks Mom is broken. Even if we all know it's true.

"Oh my poor little Pauline." Grandma Nora puts her arms back around Mom and pulls her close. "You were always such a sweet, sensitive little thing. So full of love and so easily hurt. But haven't you figured it out yet? You are broken. I'm broken, too. We all are. The whole world is broken, and sometimes I think we just crash through life, breaking each other worse."

I wait for Mom to argue, to tell Grandma Nora that she's wrong, that we're not all broken. I'm not. My room is clean. I have friends. I keep my secrets. I do well in school. I am not broken.

As usual, Mom disappoints me. She just sits, her face turned toward Grandma Nora so that I can see her profile. Her mouth is twisted, like she ate a snail and can't decide if she's going to chew it up or spit it out.

When Mom fails to reply, Grandma Nora tightens her grip and plants a kiss on Mom's sweaty forehead, just like she kissed Leslie in the kitchen yesterday morning. It's tender and it smacks of love and it's the complete opposite of the battlefield I expected to find.

And for the first time, I see them differently. For the first time, I realize what it means that Mom is Grandma Nora's daughter. I've always known that Grandma Nora is my mom's mom. I'm not stupid. It's just that I never really thought much about my mom as a person outside of my existence. I've never really thought about her relationship with her mom, except to notice when they fight. And I've never really thought about what it would have been like to grow up with Grandma Nora and Aunt Jill.

No wonder Mom is a little nuts. She spent half her life with Mrs. Fix-It and Ms. Big-Shot Real Estate Agent, who apparently got a master's degree with the money Grandpa George left Mom for art school. I knew there was some big explosion over Grandpa George's will, but this is the first time I've ever heard about my mom taking classes, and the first time I've realized that she might have wanted to do something like that. That maybe she wanted to be more than my mom.

When Mom still doesn't say anything, Grandma Nora continues to hug her. They sit in the same unnatural silence I heard before. A breeze stirs the trees, making patterned leaf shadows dance across the wooden beams of the porch. The sky is blue and deep. No clouds in sight. Warm, but not hot. Another of the Glorious Days. And I can't enjoy it.

I sit there and watch, growing uneasy and uncomfortable as the quiet stretches on. In this moment, they are more than my mom and my grandma, more than a mother and her daughter. They are Pauline and Nora, Nora and Pauline. Two people. That's all they are. Two people who look every bit as lost and confused as Leslie on those nights when I tell her she can't sleep in my room.

I pull myself back to my feet. There is a prickling feeling at the back of my neck. Aren't adults supposed to be the ones in charge? Shouldn't they have the answers?

And that stuff about being broken is bugging me. I can feel it taking root. I can feel where it will fester and become an Unanswered Question. The kind of thing capable of keeping me awake at night when I am overtired and can't turn my brain off. Niggling doubts. Bad memories. Questions like the Forbidden Room. I really do wonder what she's keeping in there. All the family's old shoes?

I shake my head to clear it. I have things to do. It's still silent when I make my way back to Leslie's room, equipped with crackers and peanut butter and grape jelly and a pair of yellow gloves.

An hour later, World War III is back in full swing.

I actually find the noise comforting. Slamming doors and clinking pickle jars are more familiar than eerie or eloquent silences. And as Tuesday comes to an end, I manage to feel cautiously happy (as far as Leslie's room is concerned, anyway). Without the stuffed animal and doll heaps, the pathways between piles are more obvious. When the trash bags are gone, we'll be able to see a huge patch of Leslie's floor.

Late that night, as Leslie and I brush our teeth, she asks me if she can take Wednesday off. At first I think she's making a bad joke, like I'm some kind of taskmaster or something.

"No!" I say. "Request denied. What do you think this is? Summer vacation?"

Leslie's eyes grow wide, and she looks surprised, even hurt.

I spit in the sink and try again.

"Leslie," I say. "I'm teasing. We worked really hard yesterday and today. It's your room. If you want a break, we can take a break."

"Oh good. I didn't want you to be mad at me, but I didn't want to hurt Dylan's feelings either."

"Leslie Anne, who is this Dylan kid? Are you hiding a boyfriend from me?"

"No," she says, but she blushes. Actually blushes.

"You're turning red. You've got a boyfriend." I start to hum: "Sitting in a tree, k-i-s-s-i-n-g." I'm rinsing my toothbrush while I hum, and Leslie goes to spit one more time. Her mouthful of foam lands on my hand. "You did that on purpose!" I grab the soap and start scrubbing.

She sprints from the room, laughing while I'm stuck at the sink washing.

I catch up to her a few seconds later and leap onto the bed next to her.

"Dish," I say.

Leslie rolls her eyes, but she's smiling. "You sound so dumb when you talk like that."

"Like what?"

"When you say things like 'dish.' You sound like you're trying to be trendy or like you're trying to be someone else."

I am actually offended. Mostly because I have a sneaking suspicion that she's right. "Dish" is one of Rae's favorite commands. So I whack Leslie with my pillow and say, "Tell me about Dylan, or I'll tell Chad you have a boyfriend."

"No. Don't do that. Dylan is not my boyfriend. We're only ten, and anyway I did tell you about him before."

"What? You did? When?"

"Remember the new kid? The one who came just before the end of school, so he could make some friends for the summer?"

"The weird kid?"

"He's not really weird. Anyway, we figured out he lives near here. He's got an aboveground pool and his mom is cooking hot dogs. Some of his cousins are coming, too. Do you wanna come? Dylan said I could bring friends."

"Nah," I say. "Too close."

"What?"

"I don't want to get to know any of our neighbors. It breaks one of my rules."

"But, Annabelle, just because they live in your Five-Mile Ra-Radish, that doesn't mean—"

"Radius."

"Five-Mile Radius. It doesn't mean that you can't be friends with them."

"Leslie, you know you don't want anyone to come over here either."

"Well, no. But that doesn't mean we can't be friends."

"It does to me."

"But what'll you do all day?" And I hear the question she's really asking: *Will you be okay with Mom and Grandma?*

"I'll be fine," I say. "I've got a new book."

"Oh, well, all right then," Leslie says. "If you're going to read, it doesn't matter where I am."

It's true. I've gotten rather spectacularly good at hiding from my life in a book, for all those times I can't physically get away. I don't talk about books with Rae or the others, but every now and then Amanda loans me one. That's another secret.

"Just don't clean up without me," Leslie says. "I want to help decide what to keep and what to throw away."

"No problem," I say. I don't mind taking a day off. Not at all.

So I go to bed feeling pretty good about life. The feeling lasts until just after 2:49 p.m. the next afternoon. That's when my entire world comes crashing down. And it's all Leslie's fault.

Wednesday is the first day that actually feels like summer. Freedom. No chores or responsibilities hanging over my head. I sleep in, and by the time I wake up, Leslie has already gone off with her friend. I eat breakfast in bed, which sounds luxurious and all, but really it's an act of survival. I planned ahead last night and brought my battlefield rations upstairs after Mom and Grandma Nora were done fighting for the day. An apple and a Pop-Tart isn't the healthiest breakfast I've ever had, but when it comes without a side of drama, it's good enough for me.

While I munch on my apple, I scroll through my phone. I neglected my messages horribly while I was cleaning. There are texts from Rae, Amanda, Jenny, and Melanie. It's nothing too exciting. Amanda says she just finished the companion to the book she loaned me, and it's just as good as the first book. Jenny is bored. Rae wants to know when we can hang out again. Melanie texted that her mom bought her neon-orange flip-flops for Family Camp. Melanie hates neon colors. She says they hurt her eyes. I'm still undecided on the issue of neon. But I am decided on this: I wish my biggest problem boiled down to the color of my flip-flops.

Then I notice that Drew's name is there, in the list of recent messages. I tap on it.

"Hey Belles," it says, and I get a little flutter somewhere between my heart and my stomach. A nickname. He's calling me a nickname. "Miss seeing you at school. Text me when you get this. There's something I want to ask you."

He's going to ask me to be his girlfriend. I know it. With Dad gone and the house caving in around us and Mom waging World War III against Grandma Nora, I needed one good thing in my pathetic summer. He's it. This is my one good thing.

I tap out a quick reply and hit send before I can second-guess myself. Then I sit there and stare at my phone, willing an answer to appear. It doesn't. When I've stared at my phone for nine endless minutes, I tell myself to stop being a loser.

I take a long shower and list all the reasons that Drew hasn't replied yet. After all, I didn't see his message for an entire day. He could be watching TV, or playing video games or, maybe, his mom is making him mow the lawn. When I get out of the shower, he still hasn't answered. I spend forever getting dressed. Because I can. And because I want to look really, really cute if today is the day an awesome, amazing, adorable guy asks me to be his girlfriend. Okay, I'm making even myself sick. I have to stop.

I braid my hair in a fun, new way that Rae taught me, sneaking fewer glances at my phone than I did before. Then I tiptoe to my room and do a quick sweep. There isn't time for the entire ritual: I don't want Grandma Nora to come upstairs and catch me digging around under the mattress. She might get the wrong idea about me. I do not want to give her a reason to think I need fixing. Like my mom.

But I do manage to check if my room is any more cluttered since I last looked. It's just something I have to do. Have to, have to, have to.

Once I determine that my room is in decent condition, I grab the book Amanda loaned me and my phone. Then I stop by the linens room to snatch an old quilt. We only have about a hundred and fifty of them. Finally, a plus to living in my mom's house. Outside, it's perfect. All my problems feel less problematic out where the sun is shining and the sky is bright and the trees are whispering in the breeze.

I settle into a comfy spot on the blanket with my back to the second-biggest cottonwood in our front yard, then I crack the book's spine and lose myself. It's a process. A little bit like falling asleep. Sometimes it's hard to find that happy other-world, but other times you can slip right into it. Like those nights when you close your eyes and you're asleep in a moment. This book is really good, and it's not long before I'm hanging out with royalty and dragon slayers and would-be poisoners. I'm a million miles away from mint-green muu-muus and spiky red hair and dads who don't call and boys who don't text back.

I have no idea how much time has passed when I finally stand and stretch. I'm hungry and I need a bathroom. I start back toward the house, leaving my stuff by the tree. Unless I can get Grandma Nora to take me to a restaurant in town (like she offered the other night), I'm going to come back out here and read away the rest of the day. Halfway to the house, I realize it's been hours since I looked at my phone. I almost go back for it, but decide to play it cool. It'll still be there after I've gone to the bathroom.

I leave the front door wide open. A little fresh air and sunshine aren't going to kill anyone in the family crypt. I stand just inside the entryway, at the foot of the stairs, and peer into the linens room, straining to see the time blinking on the cable box. I could just walk over to it, but that seems like a lot of effort. I've just decided that it's 2:49 p.m. when Grandma Nora comes down the stairs. She pauses on the second-to-last step. Her red spikes are fuzzy and unkempt. I notice her fingers are missing some of their rings.

"There's my girl," she says.

"Hey, Grandma, how's it going?"

She shrugs. "Your mother finally agreed to throw out the egg cartons with odd-numbered expiration dates." She sighs and plops down on a step, patting the spot next to her. I take the hint and sit down.

Now that I see her up close, I swear there are circles around her eyes that weren't there before. She looks like she could use a vacation, and she's only been here since Sunday. Welcome to my life, Grandma Nora. Welcome.

"We took them out to the recycle bin this morning," she says.

"What are the chances they'll still be out there tonight?"

Grandma Nora gives a dry laugh. "I'd say about fifty-fifty. For someone so stubborn, your mother sure is wishy-washy when it comes to getting rid of things."

We sit in a companionable silence for a couple of minutes. I'm trying to think of a tactful way to invite myself out to dinner on Grandma Nora's dime, but I must have a strange look on my face, because Grandma Nora cocks her head to the side and asks: "Something on your mind?"

"I heard you and my mom talking yesterday." I'm caught off guard by my own words.

Grandma rubs a hand across her forehead. "What?"

"Out on the porch."

She drops her hand and looks me in the eye. "About the will?"

"No." I shake my head. "No, you were talking about being broken."

"Oh." Grandma Nora relaxes a little. The crease between her eyebrows disappears. "What about it?"

"Well . . ." I say. I thought I had pushed that worry down, but here it is popping out of my mouth first chance it gets. "I was just wondering . . . what you said yesterday; you didn't mean it, did you?"

Grandma Nora leans back with her elbows resting on the step above her. She tilts her head to the side and appears to be trying to remember the conversation. After a longish pause, she says, "I meant every word."

"But that stuff about everyone being broken, you were just saying that to make Mom feel better. Right? 'Cause she's messed up and we're not."

"Nope, I'm afraid I meant it. All of it."

"But you don't actually think you're broken, do you?"

"Annabelle." She says my name like it's a sigh. "When I stop long enough to think about it, to really think about it, I might just be the most broken person I know."

"Why?" I ask in disbelief. Mrs. Fix-It? Mrs. Independent Woman? Is this even my grandma? Or has the real Nora

144

Perkins been abducted by little green aliens and replaced with this disheveled stranger? I just stare at her.

She blinks at me. Then she shakes her head. "Mistakes." She shakes her head again. "I've made so, so many mistakes. I've been cruel when I should have been kind. I've been greedy when I should have been giving. I . . . I didn't treat your mother very well after Grandpa George died. I was so consumed with my own grief that I didn't see how she was hurting or how I was hurting her. They're the kind of mistakes that chip away at you and leave you broken, and the only thing you can do is hope and pray you'll find a way to make it right again."

And then my mouth is moving, blurting out more of the things I thought I had tucked carefully away: "But—but you don't think everyone is broken."

"Actually, I do. Some mistakes are worse than others, but we all carry chips in our souls from the wrong we've done."

She's scaring me. Adults aren't supposed to talk like this. They're supposed to be sure and certain, confident and reassuring. Instead, she's freaking me out.

So I insist: "Not me. I'm not broken."

Grandma Nora smiles indulgently, like I'm a child. Like she knows something I don't. "You're so young, so sure of yourself." Then, still smiling, she adds: "Sometimes you remind me so much of your mom. You two are so alike."

Something inside me snaps. I jump to my feet. "I'm nothing

like my mom! Nothing like her. Don't ever say that again."
I realize I'm shouting the words, but I don't stop. Can't stop.
"I'm nothing like her. How could you even say that?"

I hear a choking noise and look in the direction of the
sound. Mom is standing a few feet away, on the other side
of the Beanie Baby Banister. At some point during our conversation, she must have walked out of the kitchen and down
the hall toward the linens room, toward the stairs where I'm
towering over Grandma Nora.

"Wh-what's going on in here?" Mom says.

I should apologize. Stop screaming. Sit down. But I can't.
All the thoughts I've been so carefully boxing up and pushing
away are popping up. I thought I could ignore them. But here
they are. From my place on the stairs, I turn my total attention to the woman who's made my life a misery.

"I'm not like you!" I shout at my mom. "I'd rather die than
grow up to be anything like you."

"Annabelle—" Her voice is choked. "Stop. Don't say things
like that."

"Like what? That you're dirty? And lazy? And—"

"Stop. Please, stop it." It's not a command. It's a plea. She's
begging, but I can't stop. And her next words—in that same
desperate, begging voice—only fuel my rage. "I'm your mother.
You shouldn't talk to me like this."

"You never act like a real mom. You just lie around and
say you're tired and obsess over your stupid collections and

I am nothing like that. Nothing. You're ruining our family, and I hate you for it. I hate you."

"Annabelle, that's enough." Grandma Nora's voice is low and harsh. I look down at her, but she's not looking at me. She's staring straight ahead—a ninety-degree angle to my position on the step. I follow her gaze and, for the first time, I notice that three more figures have joined our little party. They stand silhouetted in the front doorway. My first thought is to wonder who will show up next. Santa Claus? The Easter Bunny? The Grim Reaper? Then my eyes adjust to the back-light, and I see who they are.

This is so much worse than my mom walking in on my conversation with Grandma Nora.

Leslie is positioned in front. Her face is pale, drained of all color, but I hardly spare her a thought. Because one of the people behind her is the last person in the world I want to see at my house. The last person in the world who should see me like this: standing on a staircase lined with Beanie Babies in a house that stinks like rotten milk, screaming that I hate my own mother.

The Five-Mile Radius has been smashed to pieces.

Drew is on my front porch.

How much did he hear? How much can he see?

The questions circle round and round in my mind. I can't focus. I can't speak. I can only stand there. Someone should alert WebMD: The first death by embarrassment is about to happen. My cheeks burn, but my hands feel cold. I can't quite seem to remember how to breathe. My stomach has disappeared. And my brain keeps going back to the one thought.

How much did he hear? How much can he see?

At some point, I realize I am frozen with my finger jabbing out toward my mom. I slowly lower my hand and swallow. I try to think. Do I apologize? Pretend it was a joke? Try to laugh it off? Explain things? Tell the truth? Confess the secrets I've been keeping? I don't think I can.

How much did he hear? How much can he see?

The awkward silence stretches on and on. Why doesn't somebody say something? Why doesn't one of the adults do something? What good are they if they can't take control at a time like this? I swallow again and feel that my throat has gone tight. Great. Just great. Even if I did know what to say, I wouldn't be able to say it without bursting into tears—the one thing guaranteed to make this horrible little situation even more horrible. I try to swallow again.

"I guess we better go."

It's not an adult who finally breaks the awful, awful silence. It's the only person I don't know. For the first time, I concentrate on the third figure in the doorway. He's young. If I had to guess, I'd say he was about Leslie's age, but he looks a lot like Drew.

My brain unfreezes, and it all comes together in one catastrophic flash.

Dylan, the new kid from Leslie's class, whose cousins were coming for a cookout. Drew's cousin who just moved near us. How could I have missed it?

Of course Dylan is Drew's cousin.

Of course my life would unfold like a tragic coincidence from a Shakespeare play.

Of course Drew wasn't asking me to be his girlfriend. He probably wanted to ask the same thing that he asked on Sunday: Can he stop by my place?

Five-Mile Radius. Five-Mile Radius. Five-Mile Radius.

"Thanks for walking me home," says Leslie in a quiet voice.

"No problem." Drew speaks for the first time. "Good to see you, Annabelle." He gives me a little nod. I don't respond. I just stand there and wonder if he thinks I'm a terrible person and what he will tell other people and what if everyone finds out about our house and what if someone calls CPS or forces us to split up?

When I fail to show any sign of life, Drew doesn't say anything else to me. He turns to Leslie and says, "Later." Then he and his cousin hightail it off our porch as fast as they can without breaking into a run. I've heard speed walking is an Olympic sport. Drew and his cousin should join Team USA. I think I could guarantee a gold, as long as they thought they were fleeing from something horrifying . . . like me screaming at my mom in a house full of garbage.

I watch them go and feel my hopes slipping away. Drew has seen me at my worst. And he's seen our house. No more boyfriend. No more friends. He'll say something to someone who will let it slip to someone else who will tell someone else. By the time school starts, everyone will know I'm the kind of person who gets made fun of. Or who everyone feels sorry for. Or both. I'll be lucky if Rae or Melanie or even Amanda is still willing to be seen with me in public.

I hear a rustling noise. I tear my eyes away from the front

door in time to see Mom lumbering toward the kitchen. Without a word. After everything, after all that—she's just running away. She doesn't even care enough to keep arguing with me. To fight back. To act like she wants to save our family.

I turn on Leslie.

"What were you thinking?" Leslie looks at me with big forlorn eyes, but just now the Bambi Thing has no effect whatsoever. "Well?" I say, wanting her to defend herself. To fight with me. Something. "What were you thinking?"

"I'm so sorry." She mouths the words. I barely hear them.

"Like that matters. This is why I told you not to hang out with our neighbors."

"I'm sorry."

"This is all your fault." My throat is going tight again.

"Stop it!" Grandma Nora pulls herself up so she's standing next to me on the step. "Don't you dare blame Leslie," she says, poking me in the chest. "If you're going to act like a spoiled brat, you'd better be prepared to get caught at it."

I take a deep breath and try to relax so that I can speak without my voice shaking. "But she knows. She knows I never let anyone from school near our house. We don't have anyone over. Ever."

"I—I tried to stop him," Leslie says, still very quiet. "I really did."

"Don't talk to me." I grind out the words and stomp

upstairs, away from Doe Eyes and Grandma Nora. I pause at the top of the stairs. I want to go to my bedroom, where it's peaceful and orderly, but my room is full of Grandma Nora's stuff.

I can hear her talking to my sister. "It's okay," she's saying. "It's not your fault. She'll get over it."

I want to shout that I'll never get over it. That this will haunt me until the day I die. But it does sound like something a spoiled brat would say, and my throat is so tight I don't think I can get the words out.

"No, don't go after her," Grandma Nora is saying. "Your mother used to pull this when she was Annabelle's age, and she always needed time to cool down afterward."

I run to the bathroom and try to slam the door behind me. I want it to bang. For once, I'm not worried about causing an avalanche. Part of me is hoping I will start one. Right now, I wouldn't mind if the entire house collapsed on all of us. But the only thing that happens is that a wad of junk mail blocks the door and I have to kick a bunch of envelopes out of the way before I can slam it shut.

I sit on the toilet seat and turn on the shower, so no one will hear me if I cry. I don't. It takes a while before my throat loosens and I can breathe evenly again. Eventually, the tight feeling goes away without any tears, and I decide it's safe to leave the bathroom. When I emerge, the house is quiet and gloomy. It's late in the afternoon, and the sun is low in the sky.

I wander from room to room. The upstairs is empty. For a minute I think I'm alone. Then I hear a thudding noise downstairs, and I guess that Mom is poking around.

I try to decide what to do and where to go. I can't sleep in my room tonight. Or in Leslie's room. I stumble into Chad's room, wishing I knew if he's planning to sleep at home or if he's going to crash on Will's futon.

Chad's room is almost as creepy as Leslie's catacomb, with its stacks of exercise equipment and paint cans. That's when my eyes land on the tent.

I think of the Glorious Day outside. Fresh air and open spaces. No people. No collections. I scrounge around and find a few more supplies. I lug it all downstairs and pause at the linens room entrance when I hear the TV. Mom is parked on the couch, watching an infomercial. We have a juicer, a couple of food dehydrators, a humidifier, and I know I saw at least three ShamWows up in Chad's room just now. So much for the cleanup. I wonder what Mom is going to order today for "only five easy payments of $29.99."

I set down the camping gear and brace myself for another shouting match, but Mom doesn't protest when I switch off the TV. She's asleep. I take the batteries out of the remote so when she wakes up she'll be that much less likely to order a home rotisserie. If she hasn't already ordered one. Or five. The phone isn't next to her on the couch, so I choose to take that as a good sign. There's an ice pack half falling off her right knee. I move it to the floor before she ends up with frostbite. She should know better than to fall asleep with an ice pack. I leave her there and return to the entryway, where I gather up my camping gear.

"I've made a decision," I tell the mostly abandoned house. "I'm moving out."

The only reply I get is the faint chirping of a lonely cricket. "No, don't try to stop me. It'll only be for a day or two. Or until Grandma Nora leaves."

The cricket chirps again.

"Shut up, Jiminy," I say, and stalk outside.

I find a nice flat space behind the garage, surrounded by a little grove of young aspen trees. After clearing the space of any big rocks, I set up my tent. It's a one-man and surprisingly easy to put up. It smells stale and a little cigarette-y. I suspect this was one of Mom's yard sale spectaculars, but other than a hole or two, the tent is in pretty good shape. I fetch my things from the foot of the tree on the other side of the house, and by the time the sun starts going down, I'm ending the day the same way I started it: eating Pop-Tarts alone in bed. Only this time, bed is a sleeping bag and blanket in the backyard.

For protection, I also have a flashlight and my phone. The phone is off. I'm too much of a coward to see if anyone has called or texted me since the Stair Incident. But if that freaky woman from Rae's horror movie finds my campsite, at least

I'll be able to call the police before Mrs. Voorhees hacks me to pieces.

As it gets dark, I click on the flashlight for comfort and so I can keep reading. Amanda's book is just as good as it was this morning, but tonight I'm having a harder time losing myself in the story. I hear sounds that I might not normally notice: more crickets chirping, a car, a bird in one of the aspens, airplanes overhead. But it's the other echoes that hold me hostage to reality: I keep hearing the words I yelled at Mom and seeing the stricken look on Leslie's face and watching Drew's back as he racewalks off our porch.

Then I hear footsteps.

Startled, I drop the flashlight and the book I was reading. I scramble for my phone. But with the blanket, sleeping bag, pillow, and Pop-Tart wrappers littering my tent, I can't find it anywhere. How can I even lose something in a space this small?

The footsteps come closer. It's probably not an ax murderer, I tell myself. Then again, isn't that what everyone thinks right before they're chopped to bits? My hand collides with hard plastic. I snatch up my phone and jab down on the power button.

"Who's there?" I call.

No answer. And let's face it: No answer is just about the worst answer. It leaves room for all sorts of imagination. Then there's scratching on the tent.

That's when I panic and, in my deepest voice (which actually isn't very deep at all), I shout: "I'm calling the police."

"No! Don't do that." The front flap is pulled partially open, and Leslie's face appears in the gap. "Are you okay?" she asks. "Is something wrong with your voice?"

"No," I say in my normal tone, "I'm just glad it's you."

I didn't think someone from the house would actually check on me, but I should have known Leslie would. And that bothers me, because if she was the one pouting in the backyard, I don't know if it would occur to me to check on her. At least not right away.

"Really?" Leslie perks up. She climbs the rest of the way into the tent, saying, "I thought you were mad at me."

"I am still mad at you," I say. "I meant I'm glad in an I'm-glad-you're-not-an-ax-murderer kind of way."

"Oh." She turns to pull something into the tent after her and to zip the flap, but not before I see her expression fall. "I brought you my leftovers." She holds up a Styrofoam container.

"What?"

"Grandma Nora took me to Marcini's for dinner."

As if I didn't already know how the universe feels about me. I was going to ask Grandma Nora to take me out, and instead Leslie got to go while I was sitting in the bathroom, trying not to cry. When I don't reach out for the container, Leslie says, "It's your favorite."

I take it from her and pop it open. "You don't even like mushrooms," I say.

"But you do."

"Sometimes I hate you so much." And we both know what I really mean is "Sometimes I hate that I can't hate you."

"I hate you, too," she says.

I use my fingers to start shoveling whole ravioli into my mouth.

Leslie takes a deep breath. "I tried to warn you we were coming. I really did." She looks down where her index finger is tracing little patterns on my sleeping bag. Her fingernail makes a soft scratching sound on the nylon.

I have to finish chewing before I can reply. "It doesn't matter. You should have listened when I told you why I didn't want to be friends with people who live so close. And no matter what, you shouldn't have let Drew come anywhere near the house."

"I didn't."

"Really? 'Cause it kinda seems like you did."

"Really." She stops scratching on the bag and leans forward, looking directly at me. "As soon as he figured out that I'm your sister, Drew was super excited. He kept asking if you wanted to come over and what you were doing. And then when it was time to go, he told Dylan's mom that he would walk me home. I tried to talk him out of it, but he wouldn't listen. He really wanted to see you—"

157

I doubt he'll ever want to see me again after today.

I drop a mushroom back in the box. "Leslie, this isn't making me feel better."

"But," she says, "I texted you like a hundred times that we were coming. I thought you could meet us on the drive-way or something, and when you didn't text back, I told Drew he would have to wait on the porch. I knew you wouldn't really want him to see the porch 'cause of all the stuff out there, but it was the best I could do. Except when we got to the house, the front door was open."

"I know," I snap, angry because I'm the one who left the door open.

"Anyway," Leslie says in a littler voice this time, "I am sorry."

I don't want her innocent explanations or her sympathy ravioli or her guilt trips and big eyes.

"Oh, go away," I say.

"Can't I stay out here with you? Mom brought all the odd-numbered egg cartons back inside while we were at Marcini's, and now Grandma's so mad that she's throwing out *all* the egg cartons while Mom's asleep."

"No," I say.

"But I don't want to be in there when Mom wakes up."

"Leslie. Please just leave me alone."

And she does.

I'm not really sure why I can't let her stay. I'm as mad at

myself as I am at her. I finish the ravioli, which doesn't make me feel a whole lot better about the person I'm shaping into. While I was setting up a tent in the backyard so I wouldn't have to share a room with her, Leslie was ordering my favorite dinner—a meal she doesn't even like—so she could bring me the leftovers. I wish that she was more of a jerk. Or that I was less of one.

Between bites of mushroom and noodle, I start to think about what Leslie said. As much as I don't want to, I can't help it. I check my phone. I have thirty-three missed texts. I am never silencing or ignoring my phone again. Ever, ever again.

Five texts are from Melanie. (She and her mom won a karaoke competition—I can tell she's excited but trying not to sound excited about it.) One is from Amanda. (Have I started her book yet?) Two are from Jenny. (She made a pot at her rec-center art class, a very lopsided pot if the picture is anything to go by.) So far so good. None of them mention the Stair Incident.

Fifteen of the texts are from Leslie. Twelve are warnings that Drew is on his way.

Seven are from Drew. I have to force myself to look at them:

> **Visiting my cuz on Rainbow Rd. Can you come?**
> **Hey, your sister is here. You should come, too.**
> **ARE YOU THERE?**

Bringing your sis home. See you soon.

At your driveway.

Sorry we came at a bad time.

ARE YOU OK?

The remaining texts are from Rae. Unlike the others, she has heard about the Stair Incident. I scroll through her messages. I feel like I've been swallowing rocks instead of mushroom ravioli. I don't think Rae ever means to be mean, but Rae and her family are the definition of normal, and she expects other people—especially her friends—to be normal, too. But outside of school or when I hang out at Rae's house, there's not a lot that's "normal" about my life.

The gist of Rae's texts is that Drew told her what happened and he's really worried about me and call her, call her, call her. Why haven't I called her yet?

It's probably good that I turned on my phone. If I take too much longer to call Rae, she might contact the National Guard. Or, more likely, she'll start calling all our other friends. If she hasn't already, that is. No, they would all be texting me about it if she'd told them what happened this afternoon.

I wonder exactly what Drew told her, and I wonder how much of the house he could see. The furniture on the patio. The Beanie Babies on the stairs. Probably a little of the linens room. Definitely the sheets in the front window. Could he smell the spoiled milk?

160

Time for damage control.

Rae answers on the second ring: "Annabelle, is that you? What's going on?"

"Not much."

"That's not what Drew said."

I know it's silly, but I feel a little betrayed that they were talking, even if they were talking about me. I didn't even know he had her number. Rae is really pretty. And good at flirting. Most guys like her better than me.

"What did he tell you?" I try to sound casual, but I need to know what she knows before I can decide how to handle this.

"He said that your house is weird."

"Weird how?"

"Weird messy. How come you never told me?"

There are just some things you don't tell other people. Rae only moved to Chatham when we were in fifth grade, so she doesn't remember my family before things fell apart. If they ever thought about it, some of my other classmates might be able to guess that something bad happened to my family. Or the people we used to go to church with might be able to guess. Or the friends who used to come over before I turned ten. Like Amanda.

But the thing is, when people start asking questions you don't want to answer, it's really easy to distract them. Just play it cool—if you let them know that what they're asking about is a big deal, they might not let it go. But if you act like what they're asking about isn't life-shattering, you can change the subject. It's super easy. People spend way more time obsessing over themselves than they spend thinking about anyone else, so you just ask them something about their lives and they'll forget about yours fast enough.

"Are you still there?" Rae's voice comes across the line, sounding uncertain.

"Yeah," I say.

"I thought we were best friends," she says.

"We are." And I find myself wanting to say all the things I've never said before. To unburden myself before it comes out in another angry fit. I thought I was keeping friends by keeping my secrets, but now I wonder if I've only kept my friends away.

"Then dish," she says.

"First tell me what else Drew told you."

"Just that your house was messy and that you were fighting with your mom."

"I can't believe he saw that."

"Why?"

"I wasn't just fighting with my mom. I was screaming at her."

"Annabelle, everyone loses it with their mom sometimes. I fight with my mom all the time. It sucks that he heard you, but it's not that big of a deal. You're not a terrible person. It just makes you normal."

And that's enough. It all comes out. Right now, I need someone I'm not related to. She wants to listen, and I need to talk. At the moment, I can't think of a better definition of a friend than that. I tell Rae everything. I mean everything. I tell her the things my family doesn't even talk about with each other. All my untold truths gush out, like the filter between my mouth and my brain is MIA: the Death Files and Dad leaving and Grandma Nora coming and all the fighting and Drew showing up and me moving into a tent. I even tell her about the Five-Mile Radius.

"Wow," she says as I'm wrapping it up. By now it's so late that even the crickets are quiet. "I had no idea. So what are you gonna do? Sleep outside the rest of the summer?"

"No. I don't know. Maybe. Do you have a better idea?"

"I'll talk to my mom."

"No!"

"What? Why not?"

"I don't want her to know. I don't want anyone to look at me like that."

"Like what?"

I pause, searching for the word.

"Like I'm broken," I say.

"All right. What if I just tell my mom that things are bad for you at home right now?"

"Why do you need to tell her anything?"

"Because she's my mom," Rae says, and I wonder what

it would be like to have a mom like that, the kind you tell things to.

"If Drew calls you again, will you tell him that I don't want people to know?"

"Why don't you tell him yourself?"

"I can't. I don't know if I can ever face him again."

"Chicken."

A few minutes later, I'm saying goodbye and about to hang up when Rae stops me. "Hey, Annabelle?"

"Yeah?"

"You really never told anyone else?"

I shake my head, then remember that she can't see me. "No," I say. "I haven't ever told anyone else. Just you."

"Cool."

We hang up after that. I'm feeling better than I have since the Stair Incident. I yelled at my mom and was mean to my sister. Drew saw me having an epic temper tantrum and Grandma Nora thinks I'm a spoiled brat. But there's at least one person in the universe who knows everything and still likes me. "You're not a terrible person," Rae said. And even if she's the only one who thinks so, at least there's one. I can live with that.

Here's what I can't live with: sleeping in a tent in the backyard. It's freezing even in the middle of summer. My sleeping bag is warm enough, but my face and nose grow cold as the night wears on. It's also super creepy.

All night long, I hear strange sounds, and every time I hear something, I'm convinced it's a psycho killer from one of Rae's movies. And then there are all the rocks. I thought I got them out of the way when I was setting up, but the ground is lumpy and hard. I spend the whole night waking up every ten minutes with a new pebble or tree root digging into a different part of my body.

So much for sleep. So much for moving out. Not that anyone but Leslie even noticed my dramatic gesture. I've got to move back inside. When the sun rises only hours after Rae and I hung up, I stuff a pillow over my face, trying to block out the sun and some stupid bird that sounds like it smokes a pack a day. There's no way I'll be able to survive another night out here.

I just don't know if I can survive another day in the house.

I stay stubbornly in my tent, feeling sorry for myself. I could creep back up to Leslie's room anytime, but it seems really far away, and after yesterday and the Stair Incident, I don't want things to just go back to the way they were. I don't know how long I lie there, drifting in and out of sleep, until my phone starts ringing. It's Rae.

I wake up with a vengeance, worried about why she's calling so early in the morning.

"Hello?"

"Hey, Annabelle."

"What do you want?"

"Good morning to you, too." She laughs.

"There's not much good about it," I groan.

"I talked to my mom—"

"You promised you wouldn't," I say.

She laughs again. I hate morning people.

"Relax," Rae says. "I didn't tell her anything specific, just that things are bad for you at home right now and I thought it would be good for you to get away."

"Oh, okay . . ."

"And guess what."

I chew my lip, almost afraid to ask. But Rae sounds happy. Normal. Not disgusted. Not judgmental. "What?"

"It's a good thing I talked to my mom—because she said if you need a break from your family, you can come to the lake house with us!"

I have to have heard her wrong. With all the catastrophes life has thrown at me lately, it seems too good to be true that Rae and her family would swoop in and save me like this.

"Say that again," I order her.

"Mom said you can come to the lake house with us."

"For real?"

"For real."

We talk it over. They're leaving tomorrow at, like, 3:30 a.m. Rae says it'll be easiest if I can come over today, and spend the night. That way her family won't have to stop and pick me up on their way out of town. I just need to pack and get permission from my mom. The lake house! Three weeks in a beautiful, clean home with my best friend and swimming and water-skiing and boating.

"That sounds perfect," I say.

"This is gonna be awesome! Mom says we can come get you after she goes to the dry cleaner's and stuff. It'll probably be a couple of hours."

"Okay, but you can't bring anyone else to the house. Just you and your mom."

"Deal," she says.

"And you can't come inside."

"Fine."

"Promise me you won't even get out of your car."

"Annabelle, I promise!"

Silence.

"So . . . where do you live?"

For the first time since my tenth birthday, I find myself giving a friend directions to my house.

After Rae gets off the phone, I snap into business mode. I have tons to do. I start by taking down my camp. Then I go in search of Mom. She's in the kitchen sifting through empty milk gallons. I barely finishing asking before she tells me I can go with the McKinleys. It's almost insulting how happy Mom is to get rid of me—one less person to move around her stuff.

Next I go up to Leslie's room, dreading what I have to tell her. This is the one downside to Rae's invitation. Leslie's not going to be happy, but I have to go. I know it when I see her room. "What happened?!" I ask. If I was a cartoon character from some old Disney movie, my feet would be about a mile off the ground and my eyeballs would be completely out of their sockets.

All our carefully sorted piles are gone. The dolls. The stuffed animals. The trash bags. The boxes. All our organized stacks. Gone. Strewn across the floor. Unsorted.

Leslie gives me a wobbly smile.

"What happened?" I repeat.

"Mom," Leslie says as if the one word explains everything. And, sadly, it does.

"When?" I ask. "How did she find out we were cleaning up here? Did you tell her?"

"No." Leslie shakes her head. "Last night. After Grandma Nora and I got back from Marcini's. Grandma Nora finished throwing out the egg cartons, then she went to bed. She said she had a headache. But Mom woke up and came in my room."

No wonder Mom is so eager to ship me off with Rae's family—she's seen Leslie's room. She knows what we've been up to. I stand there, hands at my sides, and let my eyes roam over the damage. The Toy Catacombs look even worse than before we started. There used to be paths between the piles. Now it's just rubble. Teddy bears and Cabbage Patch dolls are spread out everywhere. And all our boxes and trash bags are strewn among the toys. Mom must have been having one of her nuclear meltdowns to have done this: I can't find any order whatsoever to the mess.

I want to scream. I want to smash something. How could she do this to Leslie? And to me? A little part of me even wonders if this is some kind of payback for what I said about her on the stairs yesterday. But stronger than all my warring reactions is this terrible, insurmountable exhaustion. Which only makes me more determined to go. "Leslie, why did you let her do it?"

"She said she just wanted to see what we were getting rid of . . . I couldn't stop her."

"I would have."

"I know," says Leslie. "But you were in your tent. You weren't here."

"You were."

"I'm not you," Leslie says, fiddling with the hem of her shirt. "Can we fix it?"

"Yes." I plop down, grab a trash bag, and start throwing every nasty stuffed animal inside. I don't have long before I need to start packing, but I can make enough time to help with this. Leslie closes her bedroom door and joins me in the rubble. "If Mom does this again, you have to stop her," I say.

"I can if you're here."

I don't know how to answer that, so I just grunt. Then I want to crawl into a hole and die, because you know who else grunts? My mom. She grunts when she's avoiding something or when she's upset or angry or hyperfocused.

"On the bright side," Leslie says, "at least Grandma Nora threw out the egg cartons."

I barely stop myself from grunting a second time. I want to say: *Leslie, sometimes there is no bright side. Or sometimes the only bright side is a way out.* But this is so not the time to tell Leslie that I've found my way out and I'm taking it.

So I don't say anything, and we work in silence, redoing all that Mom had undone. We've probably been sorting for an hour when I find Pukey the Porpoise in the mess, but there's no giggling stuffed-animal war this time. I just silently put him in a black bag and then leave to wash my hands.

I'm not in the bathroom very long, but when I come back, disaster has struck again. Leslie is seated on her bedroom floor, surrounded by a pile of stuffed animals that I could swear we just finished sorting. Then I notice one of the throwaway bags is turned inside out.

"Did Mom come through here again?" I ask, ready to go ballistic.

"No."

"Then why did you dump out that bag?"

"I just—I just . . ." Leslie shrugs like she can't find the words. Then she holds up a small bunny. The ears are flopped over. The fur is matted and more brown than pink after being dragged too many places over too many years.

"What about her?" I ask.

"Miss Ears was in the throwaway pile," she says. "At first I thought it was Bunbun"—she glances toward the bed, where her stuffed rabbit is sitting—"and then I realized that this one is yours."

"I know. I put her there."

"But it's Miss Ears. You've had her since I was born. She and Bunbun are practically sisters."

171

"Leslie, they're just stuffed animals."

"No, they're not. You can't throw Miss Ears away." Leslie stands up and holds out the rabbit like she's going to force the stuffed animal into my arms. I take a step back and put my hands up like a criminal about to surrender to the police. Only, I'm not surrendering—I just don't want to take the rabbit.

"But, Annabelle," Leslie says when she realizes I'm not about to take it. "You used to love her so much. You can't just get rid of her."

I frown. I try to think of a reason to put Miss Ears in the giveaway bin, but she's so old and worn-out and dirty that I can't imagine anyone else would want her. Part of me wishes I could reach out and take Miss Ears from Leslie, but there's no room for her in my life. She's nonessential.

"Whose side are you on?" I ask Leslie, annoyed that she's actually tempting me.

"Side? What sides?" Leslie asks.

"My side or Mom's side."

"What do you mean?" Leslie lowers her outstretched arm. Miss Ears dangles from her hand. Leslie looks incredibly fragile and young. Like a five-year-old clutching her favorite toy by its paw. We have a picture of me, standing almost exactly like that (only I was smiling) before my first day of kindergarten.

"It's me or Mom," I tell Leslie, slowly and clearly. "If you want to hold on to everything like Mom, then fine. I'll just go pack. But if you want to get it together, then let's put this stuff back in the trash bag. And this time leave it there."

"Pack? Why do you have to pack?"

Whoops. Well, this isn't exactly how I wanted to tell her. But since the cat's out of the bag, I try to sound bright and excited, like I have no clue that this might upset her. "Rae and her mom invited me to go to the lake with them. Isn't that awesome? We're gonna water-ski and everything."

"How long will you be gone?"

"Just a couple weeks."

"Two whole weeks?"

"Closer to three."

Leslie visibly deflates. Her shoulders, her head, the corners of her mouth, they all droop. Miss Ears falls to the ground. I grab the rabbit by her foot and toss her in the trash bag. "C'mon," I say. "Let's pick this up again and then we can go over the plan for your room. That way you can keep working while I'm gone."

"Do you have to go?"

She sounds so sad that I stop what I'm doing. Do I have to go? Really have to go? I think about World War III. I think about Drew seeing me scream. I think about Dad not calling and Chad closing the bathroom door in my face. I think about giving up my room to Grandma Nora. I think about what it's like to sleep in the Toy Catacombs, and I think about what it's like to clean up after Mom destroys all our hard work.

"Yeah," I say. "I have to."

"Please don't."

"I think I'll go crazy if I stay."

Leslie stares around her bedroom. "I might go crazy if you leave," she says. I think about her nightmares and her File o' Death, and I know she needs me.

Then she says, "Annabelle, I can't do this without you."

And something inside me hardens. I cleaned out my room alone when I was her age. There was no one to help me when I threw everything out the window. If I could figure it out, so can she. "Sure you can," I say.

"No, I can't." She's shaking her head.

This is stupid. A yes-no-yes-no fight won't get us anywhere. So I say: "I promise to help you when I get back. But someday, you're going to have to learn how to stand up for yourself. You have to be strong on your own."

"I thought we were stronger together," she says.

I leave anyway.

It doesn't take me long to pack. Luckily, Grandma Nora is downstairs waging her war on the house, so I have my room to myself while I stuff my duffel bag full of shorts and T-shirts and swimsuits. It's early afternoon by the time I drag my luggage downstairs and find Grandma Nora fiddling with the doorknob of the Forbidden Room. I really do wonder what Mom is keeping in there. All the leaves Dad rakes up in the yard every autumn?

"Are you trying to pick the lock?" I ask.

Grandma Nora jerks away from the door and hides the screwdriver behind her back. She looks like a kid who just got caught stealing chocolate chips from the pantry. She glances to her right and then to her left. "Oh, is it locked? I just thought maybe the door was jammed."

And now I know where Leslie inherited her inability to lie.

I smile. "Okay then. Hey, will you tell my mom I said bye?"

"What? Where is she? Is your mother coming?" Grandma Nora takes another step away from the door. Then the second part of what I said sinks in and she focuses on me, on the duffel bag and backpack in my hands. "What's all this?" She gestures to my luggage, and I see that there are no longer any rings on her fingers. Even her nails are ragged and unkempt.

I consider answering Grandma Nora's question. I really do. But I know what she'll say. She'll say all the things my mom should have said. Grandma Nora will tell me that I should follow through on my promise to Leslie, that I should stay and help her clean. She'll tell me I should apologize to my mom for the scene on the stairs yesterday. She'll say all the things I don't want to hear. So I ignore Grandma Nora's question.

Instead, I say: "You might want to put the screwdriver away before my mom notices you had it out. You don't even want to know what happened last time my dad tried to open that door."

Grandma Nora looks like she's about to ask what happened, but a creak from the upstairs hallway sends her scurrying off. She must be as tired of fighting with my mom as the rest of us are of hearing them fight.

176

I pick up my bags, hoping to slip from the house without any more fuss. I don't make it.

"Are you leaving already?" Mom asks, descending the stairs slowly. Her knees must still be hurting.

"Yeah."

"I talked to your friend's mom on the phone." This surprises me, since I'd told Rae that Mrs. McKinley didn't need to call. "They seem like nice people."

"Yeah," I say again. "Mrs. McKinley is awesome."

And you're not.

The unspoken words hover in the air between us. My mom pauses a second and squeezes her eyes closed; it's like a slow-motion flinch. She opens her eyes again and takes the last few steps in silence. I shift my weight with my bags in hand, wishing that Rae and her mom would just show up already.

On the bottom step, Mom says, "Leslie sounds pretty upset that you're leaving. I think she's crying in her room."

It's the last thing I want to hear, especially coming from Mom.

"If she's so upset, why don't you do something about it?" I say, then I rush out the front door before either of us can say anything else. I don't stop until I reach the end of our driveway, and it's a long, long driveway. I stand there, near the main road, like a hitchhiker, and wait until Rae and her mom arrive.

— — —

As soon as we get to the McKinleys' house, Rae and I pull on our swimsuits and jump into the pool. We spend most of the afternoon lying on lounge chairs, and I love the way Mrs. McKinley brings us lemonade and snacks and reminds us to put on more suntan lotion.

"This is so fun," Rae says. "When it's just the two of us. We're definitely the closest friends in our group, aren't we?"

I'm absentmindedly nodding when Rae's mom appears with watermelon slices. "Thanks," I say.

Rae rolls her eyes. "You don't have to tell her thank you every time she brings something. She's just trying to clean out the fridge before we leave, aren't you, Mom?"

Mrs. McKinley laughs a little and rolls her eyes right back Rae. "At least someone taught Annabelle good manners."

Rae sticks out her tongue at me. So I stick out my tongue back at her. Unfortunately, I have a mouthful of watermelon and a bunch of pink mush oozes down my chin. Some of it sprays on my legs.

"Ew!" says Rae, scooting away from me on her chair, which makes me laugh. More watermelon-tinged spit sprays everywhere. Rae starts laughing, too. And once we start, neither of us can stop. Maybe the sun has fried our brains.

After a while, Mrs. McKinley seems to agree that we've gotten enough sun and she calls us inside to help. She wants to leave the house clean. It's a strange concept to me. Why bother scrubbing down a house we're not going to use for three weeks? I can totally understand cleaning after we get back . . . but before we go? It's so different from the way my family operates that it almost makes me wonder if I'll miss home. I've never been away from my family for more than a couple of nights at a time before. Three weeks is starting to sound like a long time.

Rae and I empty the dishwasher and dust the down-stairs. While we work, I keep thinking how ironic life is. I left Leslie to deal with the Toy Catacombs by herself, so I could help Rae dust her sparkling house. It doesn't make any sense.

As we finish wiping down the dust-free bookshelves, Rae pulls out her phone.

"I'm inviting Jenny over. That way Mom won't give us any more chores."

"Won't she just make Jenny help?"

"Since you're going on vacation with us, Mom's treating you like family, but Jenny's a guest."

I'm half-pleased that Rae thinks her mom is treating me like family. But the other half of me feels awful. I hate the way Chad always escapes to Will's house and leaves me to deal with Mom and the house and Leslie. How is this any different? Guilt, guilt, guilt. This is probably why I tell Rae: "I'm not really in the mood to hang out."

"Too late," says Rae, hitting the send button.

"Fine. But if Jenny is coming over, we should invite

Amanda, too." Rae gets a funny look on her face. She doesn't say no, but she doesn't say yes either. She says, "Only if she can get her own ride. My mom doesn't have time to pick up anyone else today."

"Is Jenny getting her own ride?"

"Yeah."

"Okay."

"Fine."

"Fine."

I'm not sure what just happened, but I think it might have been a fight. Or one of those weird nonfights. And I have no idea what it was about.

After Jenny and Amanda arrive, we move to the back deck, the one that overlooks the pool. Or, to be more accurate, Mrs. McKinley shoos us outside so she can vacuum a carpet that looks like it was already vacuumed once this morning.

We sit in a half circle. Rae and I are side by side on the porch swing. Amanda and Jenny sit in rocking chairs on either side of us. We talk a little about the party last weekend. I can't believe it was only a few days ago. It feels like centuries since Dad left and Grandma Nora came to visit.

Then Amanda asks if I've finished her book.

"Not quite," I say, sneaking a peek to see if Rae and Jenny are rolling their eyes at Amanda wanting to talk about books.

To my surprise, Jenny actually sets her phone aside (she's been obsessively texting Melanie since she arrived) and says, "Ooohh, what book?"

I never knew that Jenny liked to read. The one time I asked Rae which books she liked, she said, "Reading is so lame." I didn't bring it up again.

Amanda tells Jenny, "I gave Annabelle *The Hero and the Crown*."

"I loved that book," says Jenny. "I read it after Ms. Monroe told me I'd like it."

"The school librarian?" says Rae, her eyebrows almost disappearing into her hairline.

Jenny nods.

"I know," said Amanda. "And I read it because you said it was really good. Remember?"

"Oh yeah," Jenny says. They start talking about the novel, and get in this big debate about whether they like Luthe or Tor better. I have to cover my ears and shout, "Stop! Stop! Stop!" whenever they start to talk about the ending.

"But Luthe saves Aerin," Jenny is saying. "He brings her to the Lake of Dreams. Without him, she'd have died."

"So what? If you think about it, Aerin probably would have died as a kid without Tor," Amanda says. "He was her only friend, and he knows her better than anyone. He accepted her when no one else did."

Rae is sitting on one foot. She drags the other foot loudly across the wood surface of the deck as I rock us back and forth in the swing.

Jenny says, "Sure Tor knew her when she was a kid, but by the end, he doesn't know her anymore. She's different after everything she survived. I mean, when she goes after her evil uncle—"

"Stop! Stop! Stop!" I say for the third or fourth time. "I haven't gotten to that part yet."

"Okay, fine. If you're going to be all dramatic about it," says Jenny, but she's smiling.

"Who do you like better?" Amanda asks me.

"I'm not sure yet."

"Well, hurry up and finish it," says Jenny. "I know you're going to be on my side. For real." She's texting as she says this, and I assume that she's back to giving Melanie moment-by-moment updates. So it catches me by surprise when Amanda's phone chimes.

Since when did Amanda and Jenny become such good friends? I always thought Amanda hung out with our group because of me. But Chatham is a small town, and it occurs to me that Amanda has probably known Jenny for as long as she's known me. It's a little disconcerting to hear them talking like this—not as my friends but as each other's friends.

Amanda reads Jenny's message, but she doesn't text Jenny

back. She answers out loud: "No. You're wrong. Aerin has to be with Tor. She has to go back. She can't just—"

"Okay," I say, stopping the swing and the sound of Rae's dragging foot, "if you guys are so determined to ruin the end of the book for me, I'm going inside for a minute, and when I get back, you better be talking about something different."

I'm already sliding the glass door closed when it occurs to me that Rae has been strangely silent, almost pouty. Well, she was the one who wanted to have other people over. It's not my fault if she doesn't like the conversation.

Mrs. McKinley spots me crossing the living room. "Hey, Annabelle," she says, "will you remind Rae that I'm going to need you two to help with the windows after Jenny and Amanda leave?"

I nod.

"Thank you, dear." She whisks away, leaving me to wonder: What am I doing here? Washing windows? When I never do that at home?

Like a prayer, I start reciting my list of reasons for leaving. I have to remind myself that it's not optional. It's a necessity. If I stay, I'm going to go crazy. And it's not wrong to save yourself. Even if it hurts someone else. Is it?

I trudge down to Rae's room, where we left my bags. I sit on the floor and dig mindlessly through my luggage. I need a reason to stall. I need some time to sort myself out. My arm is almost completely in my bag when something fuzzy brushes against my hand. It's tucked away in the bottom corner of the bag. I don't remember packing anything that feels like this.

My hand closes around the furry object, and I pull out a matted, dirty stuffed animal. It's Miss Ears. I can think of only one way she would have gotten into my suitcase.

When I was in preschool, Miss Ears went everywhere with me. In the car. To Sunday School. The grocery store. The park. I even dragged her to the first day of kindergarten, where Bobby Jones said, "You're a baby. Only babies bring stuffed animals to school with them."

Miss Ears has sand in her bottom. It weighs her down and makes her sit up without tipping over. It also makes her really good for hitting people. You can grab her by the ears and wallop someone pretty hard with her sand bottom.

So on the first day of kindergarten, when Bobby called me a baby, I whacked him with Miss Ears. Turns out, Bobby Jones was the real baby. He sure cried like one. After that Mrs. Patterson said Miss Ears would have to stay home when

I was at school. I started carrying Miss Ears around less and less, but she kept her place of honor on my pillows. For years, I still hugged her when I cried and slept with her tucked under the blankets next to me. Until one day, I threw Miss Ears out the window.

She belongs to a different time—a time when my family was different, when Mom was happier. When Miss Ears was new and her fur was unmatted, we acted like a family. Now she's old and dirty and worn, and I can't stand seeing her, knowing Leslie hid her in my suitcase after I tried to get rid of her again. Leslie is holding on for me, even when I've been too tired to hold on for myself.

It hurts somewhere deep inside in that place that refuses to stay boxed up or shoved away. I want to throw Miss Ears out another window or toss her in the nearest garbage can. Instead, I find myself hugging her, clutching her in a death squeeze so tight I wouldn't be surprised if her seams burst and the sand in her bottom drained all over Rae's freshly vacuumed carpet. I have no idea how long I sit there, clutching Miss Ears to my chest, lost in unhappy thoughts.

Quiet giggling pulls me out of my trance.

"What are you doing?" Rae asks. She and Jenny peer into the room, and I realize they have just caught me sitting alone on the floor, hugging a stuffed animal. I toss Miss Ears back into my duffel bag. My face is in flames.

"I was just looking for my hairbrush," I say.

"That's not what it looked like," says Jenny, her eyebrows raised. There's a funny expression on her face. I can't tell if it's from concern or trying to hold back more laughter.

I don't say anything. I yank my hairbrush out of the bag in an awkward, jerky motion and start tugging it through my hair. Jenny and Rae watch from the doorway like I've lost my mind.

After a minute where the only sound is the brush pulling through my hair, Rae says, "You're acting really strange. Are you okay?"

I look at them and shrug. That's when I notice Amanda is hovering behind them. I wonder if she was giggling, too.

"Is this something about your mom?" Rae asks.

"Rae!" I say.

"What?" She looks surprised.

"You promised you wouldn't say anything." My voice is loud, louder than normal.

I'm so upset that I don't notice at first how my reaction is only making everything ten times worse . . . and ten times more interesting. Jenny's and Amanda's eyes are glued to us.

"What's wrong with you?" Rae asks. "I didn't say what her issues are. I just asked if you were acting all weird because of her."

"No. This isn't about *that*," I say. "If anything, it's about my sister."

"Your sister?" asks Rae. "She'll be fine. Leslie can survive without you for a few weeks. You told me yourself that you were practically her age when you took care of your room."

It's weird to hear Rae repeat my words. I've told myself the same thing. I've even said it to Leslie. But when I hear someone else say the words, I can hear how harsh and unfeeling they are. And that's when I know.

My decision is slow in coming. I think it through carefully, weighing what I'm about to say before I say it. I don't want to give up freedom and sunshine and three weeks of sanity. I look from Rae to Miss Ears and then back to Rae again.

"But Leslie shouldn't have to do it herself," I say. "Not if I can help her."

The words are slow to leave my lips, and my tongue feels like it weighs a hundred pounds.

"Fine," says Rae. "You can help Leslie when you get back."

I shake my head. "I can't leave her. Not now. It's a really bad time."

"Ha-ha. Very funny," Rae says, as if she's waiting for me to say, "Gotcha!"

"Rae, I think she's serious," Amanda says.

"I am," I say. "I can't go to the lake with you. I have to go home."

"I can't believe you want to go back there," says Rae. "You told me what it's like."

Jenny looks like she's about to shout, "What's it like?

What's it like?" Rae and her big mouth. She's about to give away everything.

"That's why I have to go," I tell Rae, trying to explain without really explaining in front of Amanda and Jenny. I'd ask them to leave, but Jenny's not going anywhere. She looks like the only thing she needs is a bucket of popcorn. "I can't leave Leslie to deal with it," I say.

"But it'll be so boring without you."

"I'm sorry. I wish I could go. I was planning to. I really, really wanted to . . . but something reminded me of why I have to go home. Please understand."

Rae looks at me carefully for a minute. Her gaze locks on Miss Ears, then she huffs, but to my surprise, she stops arguing. "Whatever. I guess I'll just go tell my mom you're not coming." Rae leaves without waiting for my response. Jenny trots after her. In the hallway, I can hear her ask, "What's wrong with Annabelle's mom?"

There's a pause.

I hold my breath, waiting for Rae's answer. For one horrible moment, I think she's going to betray me, to punish me for ditching her. But then Rae just says, "Never mind."

Amanda stays behind. "Are you sure you shouldn't go with Rae?"

"Ye-es?" I say, stretching the word into two syllables and making it more of a question than a statement.

"Everyone needs to run away sometimes," Amanda says.

The words are a slap. Amanda doesn't mean them that way, but they are. Because she's right. It's exactly what I was trying to do; I was trying to run away. Like Chad and Dad.

I was trying to get away from my family like it's an old and broken and worn-out stuffed animal. But Miss Ears isn't as nonessential as I thought, and it's time for me to stop watching and start doing something.

"Hey, Amanda," I say, "do you think you could drop me off at home? When your ride comes?"

I want to cry when I say goodbye to Rae. It feels like days instead of hours since we were eating watermelon by the pool. Rae barely stops talking with Jenny to wave me off, and I have to push down a little twinge of jealousy. And I also have to wonder if I've done the right thing. Should I be leaving? I'm questioning everything. I'm even questioning if I should I have stopped Rae from telling Jenny and Amanda about my family.

I told Rae my family's secret, and she was way nicer than I thought anyone would be. She didn't make fun of me. She tried to help. I've kept silent for so long that it's a habit. But I'm starting to think that I haven't helped anyone by hiding the mess at home. Maybe the silences have even made things worse—allowed the problems to fester and grow. Maybe it's time to stop keeping everything secret.

The drive home is quiet. I'm lost in thought, and Amanda seems to sense that I'm not in the mood to chat. As we near the house, I discover that I'm not quite brave enough to let them see it. I ask Amanda's mom to drop me off at the end of the driveway, where Rae and her mom picked me up hours ago. I might be rethinking my silences and the Five-Mile Radius, but I'm not quite ready to give them up yet.

I wave goodbye to Amanda and her mom. More than halfway up the driveway, I set down my duffel bag and backpack, stretch my arms wide, and try to let the rightness of coming back settle over me. The sky is blue, the clouds are fluffy, and the trees lining our drive flutter in a little breeze. I pretend they are welcoming me home. I pretend Rae isn't getting ready to go to the lake without me.

"I came back," I say.

As usual, the universe is more interested in punishing me for my misdeeds than it is in rewarding me for my good ones. The words are barely out when the breeze turns into a full-blown gust. A bunch of driveway dust flies into my wide-open mouth.

I try to spit it out, but that doesn't seem good enough. So I dig through my suitcase until I find the mouthwash. I'm gargling and spitting when Chad walks out of the garage, holding a wrench in one hand and a greasy cloth in the other.

"What are you doing, weirdo?"

I spew a minty blue patch on the gravel and walk toward him. "Do you think Listerine kills hantavirus?"

"Probably not."

I throw the bottle cap at his face. He catches it.

"Leslie said you left. Aren't you supposed to be with Rae's family or something?"

"You mean you actually talked to Leslie?"

His forehead scrunches together. "What? Why wouldn't I?"

"Oh never mind." I take another swig of Listerine, gargle, and spit. I gesture for him to hand back the bottle cap. "I'm not going anywhere," I tell him as I close the Listerine.

"Les will be glad that you decided to stick around."

"I know," I say. I'm not quite ready to break my silence with all my friends, but I decide to try it with a family member. "Just like I'd be glad if you ever stuck around."

"What are you talking about?" Chad seems genuinely surprised. "I never get to go anywhere."

"Yeah, but you're never home either." I've sat back and watched him leave every day for weeks and weeks, but I've never really said anything before. Why haven't I?

"I didn't know it bothered you," says Chad. His forehead hasn't unscrunched yet.

"Well, it does."

I start lugging my bags to the house. Chad is frozen with the same confused look on his face and his mouth half-open like he wants to say something more, but he doesn't know what. He should probably close his mouth before he swallows a bunch of dust and hantavirus.

Once inside, I hear a commotion in the den. Grandma Nora and Mom. From the sound of it, they're in the middle of the same unending, exhausting argument. I can't handle it right now. So I ignore them.

I walk straight to Leslie's room, hoping she'll be there, and I'm in luck. Her back is to the door and she's sitting in a pile of plastic toys. There is a black bag on one side of her and a box on the other side. She looks so little and alone. I drop my bags.

"Chad? Is that you?" she says.

"I'm back."

"Annabelle!" She dashes across the room, dodging toys and trash bags. She throws her arms around me. I hug her back tight and force myself to say the words before I chicken out or convince myself that they're not needed.

"I'm sorry," I say.

It's easier than I would have thought.

Leslie drops her arms and looks up at me. "You're not leaving again, are you?"

I shake my head. "No. I'm not going anywhere."

"Then why are you sorry?"

I should have known Leslie would come up with something like that. I have so much to apologize for that I don't even know where to begin. "I guess I'm sorry for . . ." *For trying to run away. For leaving when I said I'd help you clean up. For blaming you that Drew saw me screaming at Mom. For letting you live in a room that gives you nightmares.* ". . . for everything."

"Grandma Nora says it's stupid to apologize for things that aren't your fault." Leslie grabs my arm and drags me to sit with her on the bed. "Anyway, the important thing is that you came back."

"I shouldn't have tried to leave."

She shrugs. Like it's no big deal. "Dad and Chad do it all the time."

"I know," I say. "That's the problem. We have to stop leaving every time things get hard."

"I thought you said Mom was the problem," Leslie says.

I flop back on her bed, so I'm lying flat and I won't have to look at her while I admit it: "I think I might have been wrong."

Leslie flops back next to me. "I knew everything would be okay." And I promise, if eyes could light up, her Bambi eyes would be shining like stars.

Optimistic little twerp.

"So what are we working on?"

"The Choking Hazards," she says. She sits back up and gestures to the pile she was going through when I walked in. It's a mess of plastic junk: Legos and Polly Pocket pieces and Happy Meal prizes.

"Ugh," I say. I've been dreading this pile.

"I know," says Leslie. "It's taking forever."

But she doesn't sound like she minds at all. I slide to the floor and start sorting.

I feel cautiously hopeful about my decision to come home. I change my mind when Leslie and I go downstairs for a glass of water. We find Mom and Grandma Nora in the den. Grandma Nora stands with her arms full of cans—all different types of corn. Mom is standing in front of the wall of canned goods. Her arms are spread wide like she's about to take a bullet for the cans or something.

"You can't have them," she's saying.

"For the last time, I'm not taking them," Grandma Nora says. "I'm just moving them into the kitchen."

"You finished the kitchen?" I ask, surprised that Leslie didn't say anything earlier.

They jerk around to face me.

Mom drops her arms. "What are you doing here?"

"I came home."

"Good girl." Grandma Nora beams at me.

At the same time, Mom says: "Why?"

I ignore Mom and ask, "Are you really moving the cans into the kitchen?"

Mom says no at the same time Grandma Nora says yes.

They go back to their squabbling. Mom tries to snatch a can of creamed corn from Grandma Nora. She fails, but returns to her previous stance—arms spread out, protecting the green beans and sliced carrots with her body.

"The pantry's cleared out," Leslie tells me from her place at my side.

"Really? Why didn't you tell me sooner?"

"Come see."

I don't think Mom and Grandma Nora even notice that we leave. I follow Leslie to the kitchen, and I almost fall to my knees. It's magnificent. Okay, so magnificent is probably an overstatement. It's nowhere near as nice as the McKinleys', but it looks a thousand times better than it did before. Newspapers are spread all around the breakfast nook, but the other "collections" are gone. No paths, because the floor is clear. Counters are clean. There is empty space on the tops of the cupboards and there are empty shelves in the pantry. Nary a milk jug in sight.

"How? When?" I ask. I can't believe the transformation.

Then Leslie says, "Mom took a nap this afternoon and Grandma Nora got really mad and threw everything away. She made Chad help her load the truck and then she got him to drive it all into town."

"Oh." My voice is flat. All that hopefulness and trying to feel good about coming home crumbles. "So Mom didn't okay it."

Leslie shakes her head. She looks disappointed, too.

"Then it'll just get bad again," I predict, "when Grandma Nora leaves. It'll end up worse than before. Mom has to want things to change."

"I think so, too. That's why I didn't tell you sooner," says Leslie. "It's all for nothing."

It hurts to hear Leslie say something so cynical, so—so much like something I would say. There's a crash in the den.

It sounds like a bunch of cans have been knocked over. I close my eyes and try not to think about the trip to the lake. In one sentimental moment over a stuffed rabbit, I gave up my chance for sanity. What have I done?

It's hours and hours later when I wake up, confused and disoriented. In the dark, the boxes and bags and half-sorted piles of the Toy Catacombs make horrible shapes. I squeeze my eyes shut and send a request to the universe that Grandma Nora won't stay too much longer. I want my room back. I glance over at the alarm clock on Leslie's nightstand. It's just after 3:00 a.m. Usually—if I'm not in a tent in the backyard— I'm a sound sleeper, a very sound sleeper. So at first, I can't figure out what woke me.

Then I hear it.

Muffled noises come from the pillow next to mine. They grow louder and louder before tapering off again. I roll over, and what I see makes me feel as if my chest is about to crack in half.

Leslie told me she had nightmares, but seeing this is different. It's real, and it's so . . . sad. I knew she needed me, and I came back. We're cleaning her room. Leslie shouldn't be wincing into her pillow and making noises like someone has just drowned a basketful of puppies in front of her.

The whimpering turns into choking sounds. I can't just sit

here and watch this. I click on the lamp and reach out to stroke Leslie's hair. "Ssshhh, it's okay," I say in my softest, least-Annabelle-like tone. In the dim lamplight, her cheeks are damp. "Ssshhh."

But things only get worse, as they are prone to do around me.

Leslie wakes up. But it's not calm or gradual. It's sudden and violent. She bolts upright, knocking my hand away from her face with both arms. She's breathing deeply. I'm not sure if hyperventilating is the right word, but it's something close to panic. She continues to sputter and gasp.

"Breathe, just breathe," I say, making circles on her back. She's so little. I can feel her shoulder blades and her spine sticking out through the cloth of her nightgown. Then she's up and out of the bed, stumbling through the mess. "What are you d—" I start to ask, but the question is answered before I can finish asking.

She dives for one of the black bags and shoves her entire head inside. I hear her gagging. She emerges a minute later and limps back to bed, where she asks for her cup of water. I grab it from the nightstand.

When she's done drinking, I ask, "Do you think you have the stomach flu?"

This is normally the part where I freak out, where I run to the bathroom, hop in the shower, and demand that the person who may or may not have the plague stay at least sneezing distance away. But a horrible suspicion is sinking over me. Pukey the Porpoise.

"How often?" I ask, leaning toward her. "How often do you wake up sick?"

Leslie shrugs and passes me her cup, which I return to its spot between the alarm and lamp.

"How often?" This time it's not a question. It's a demand.

"Not much." She's a terrible liar.

Her skin is almost translucent in the half-light, and it could be my imagination or it could be the shadows, but I see thick dark circles under her eyes.

"Once a month?" I guess. "Once a week?"

She shakes her head and lies back down, snuggling deep into her pillow. "Not that much. Just if I've been really, really upset about something."

Like anxiety because her sister tried to abandon her? Like stress because her crummy dad ran off and didn't bother to call?

I prop myself on one elbow and stare down at her. Leslie doesn't want to talk, but I can't help it. I have to ask. I have to know what kind of dream makes a person so upset that they wake up and puke.

"What was your dream about?"

"I was trapped underwater and drowning and I kept trying"—she takes a long, shuddery breath—"I don't want

200

to talk about it. I just want to go back to sleep . . . Will you—will you hold my hand a little while?"

I hold her hand and watch her face relax. When her breathing is deep and even and I'm sure it won't bother her, I slip my hand from hers, grab the bag, and tiptoe out. I can't stop her whimpers from echoing in my head. I can't stop watching her leap for the trash bag. I can't stop thinking how pale she looked. Guilt, guilt, guilt. I thought I would feel better after coming home, but I feel worse than ever. I haven't helped Leslie, and now we're both stuck here and there's no one to turn to.

I sneak downstairs and set the trash bag outside the back door.

There's a light in the kitchen. Grandma Nora is on her hands and knees with a massive sponge, scrubbing the floors. The part of the floor she's cleaning is at least three shades lighter than the rest of the tile. I watch her work. I know where there's a mop, and I think about going to get it for her, but I change my mind as it occurs to me that this chance to talk alone with Grandma Nora couldn't be more perfect.

After what just happened upstairs, I know more than ever before that I'm in over my head. And this is an opportunity I can't pass up. Maybe Grandma Nora can actually help Leslie. Maybe she can do something to make the bad dreams stop.

"Grandma Nora," I say.

"Oh, Annabelle," she says, looking up from the floor and grabbing her shirt with a soapy hand. It leaves a big wet spot on the fabric. "You startled me. What are you doing up at this hour?"

"I just needed someone to talk to."

Grandma Nora tosses her sponge into a container of dark brown water. It's so filthy that I wonder how it's making the floor cleaner. She sits back on her heels and gives me a long look.

Poor Grandma Nora. In the dim light, her wrinkles appear deeper and darker than they do in the middle of the day. Maybe she's just not wearing any makeup, and her hip hair spikes have devolved into fuzz. Her head looks like a red baby chick exploded. But the thing is: She's here. And right now I need someone.

I say, "I'm worried about Leslie."

She nods. "Me too."

I cross the kitchen, trying to step only in the dry spots. I wonder if Grandma Nora knows about Leslie's nightmares. I wonder if, in the few days she's been in the house, Grandma Nora has noticed what the rest of us have missed—that Leslie is so anxious about the house and the mess and the tension she's making herself sick with it. Before I can ask, Grandma Nora adds, "I'm worried about you, too, Annabelle."

"Me?" I stop in a large dry spot, standing only a few feet from Grandma Nora. "Why? I'm fine."

I'm strong. I don't cry. I don't have nightmares.

"This isn't a healthy environment." Grandma Nora waves a dripping hand at the kitchen. "We've been working for days, and it's still filthy. I'm starting to realize that I can't fix your mother, but maybe I can save you and Leslie."

A little shiver runs down my spine—she's giving up on the rest of the family?

"What do you mean?" I ask.

"Aunt Jill and I have been talking about it, and we think it would be best if you came to stay with us. Neither of us has much spare room, but I could take Leslie with me, and you can stay with Jill. Her place is only about an hour across town. So we'll be able to get together on the weekends."

I cannot believe what I'm hearing. Is Grandma Nora really sitting in the middle of a partially cleaned floor at 3:45 a.m., calmly proposing to stash me at Aunt Jill's house? I barely know the woman. How can she even suggest splitting me and Leslie up?

Any plan that involves tearing apart our family is a terrible plan, and I tell her so. "That's a terrible plan. You can't split up me and Leslie. She needs me."

Grandma Nora shakes her head. "Leslie needs a healthy home, and so do you. I know it's not a perfect plan, but it will have to do for now. It's certainly better than if CPS or the government end up involved."

I take a step back. I don't think Grandma Nora means to

sound like she's making threats, but it sure sounds like she just warned me she would call CPS if we didn't agree to her plan.

"But what about Chad? And my dad?" I ask, taking another step away from her.

"Well, Chad is practically an adult. He'll be leaving for college in another year. And your father . . ." She sighs again. "If he's willing to leave your mother, then of course, you can live with him. But you can't stay in this house."

"So you want us to move out and leave Mom here?" I ask.

My mind sends me a mental image of the Death Files. And suddenly I'm sure of it: If I leave with Grandma Nora, I just know I'll open a newspaper someday and see my mom in the headlines. We can't abandon her to this house. One of her collections really will crush her to death. Mom is collapsing under the weight of the house, and Grandma Nora wants us to run out on her?

Grandma Nora just keeps shaking her head. "Look, I've given this a lot of thought. I wouldn't have said anything if I didn't truly think it would be for the best."

My world is toppling faster than a newspaper tower.

I can't tell Grandma Nora about Leslie's nightmares now. She'll call CPS, and we'll be living a thousand miles from our friends and family before Dad even bothers to pick up a phone. I thought not leaving with Rae would make things right. I promised myself that I wasn't going to run away ever again. And now I might not be running, but the one person I thought I could turn to wants to help Leslie by breaking up our family. I choke back the knot that's forcing its way up my throat.

"I'm not going anywhere," I tell her, and sprint from the room before I do something disgraceful. Like cry. In my rush, I don't see the industrial-size tuna can that never made it to the pantry. It's lying in the middle of the half-cleaned floor, and I whack my toe on it. As if Grandma Nora needs the universe to help prove her point that our house isn't "healthy."

"Annabelle, are you okay?"

I don't answer, and I don't slow down until I reach Leslie's room. I stumble back into her bed without further injury, but waves of pain that have nothing to do with my stubbed toe press down on my chest. I love my sister and my brother and my dad and my friends. I love the mountains and the cottonwoods. I can't imagine—don't want to imagine—my life without them. I even have trouble imagining my life without seeing Mom every day.

The next day (or technically later the same day), I have a hard time focusing on the job. Leslie and I are working on the Square Things, which are really in more of a wall than a pile, but it feels pointless. It's not enough. So what if we get her room clean?

Leslie isn't going to be here to enjoy it. Grandma Nora will see to that. And since Mom didn't have a say in Project Catacombs Extraction, she'll restock it first chance she gets.

And even if we do get her room clean and stay here, it's still not enough. Leslie needs more than that. She needs to not have nightmares. She needs parents who notice that she's making herself sick. She needs help. This whole family does.

Leslie pulls an Easy-Bake Oven from the pile. "I remember when Mom bought this for me!" she says, perhaps a little too brightly. "We were at a garage sale. I was too little to use it, but Mom said I could have it when I was older. Do you think I'm old enough now?"

If anything, she's getting too old for it. She can use the real kitchen if Mom or I help her (or Grandma Nora, if she drags us to another state), but I don't mention that. I just say, "Put it in the Keep Pile."

"That was a good day," she says. "The day we bought the Easy-Bake."

"Mmm-hmm." I'm not really listening. I am wondering if I am being selfish if I try to stay here with Leslie. Was it wrong of me not to tell Grandma Nora that my sister's nightmares are making her sick? I don't want to live with Aunt Jill, but maybe it is better for Leslie. Maybe she should go with Grandma Nora, and I can stay. After all, my room is clean. But then Leslie and I would live a thousand miles apart. And even if I am here to save Mom from becoming a File o' Death statistic, I might end up legitimately insane from the mess.

Every possible solution I come up with is worse than the last.

I am holding a plastic woolly mammoth in my hand, a stray Happy Meal prize from yesterday's Choking Hazards. The woolly mammoth says three different catchphrases when you press the button on its back. It still works, so I don't think I should throw it away, but why should I put it in the giveaway pile? Who would want it? (Other than my mom.)

Leslie is still chattering about her Easy-Bake Oven. She doesn't have the faintest clue that Grandma Nora is scheming to take her a thousand miles from everything she knows and loves. She wants to know what I think she should make and where do I think she can find the mixes? I don't answer. I'm frozen, like a computer that's locked up, staring at the mammoth: Throw away or keep? Throw away or keep? Throw away or keep?

I think I've lost trust in my own judgment.

"Want some help?"

The unexpected sound of Chad's voice startles me. I drop the woolly mammoth. It lands on its back button and says, "Modern architecture. It'll never last." We all ignore the mammoth.

"Chad! What are you doing here?" Leslie skips over to him.

Chad looks uncomfortable. He jams his hands into his pockets and says, "I thought I'd see if you needed another pair of hands. Just for this afternoon. I have to work tomorrow, but I'm off today." He takes a couple more steps into the room. "Yech, this place is a mess."

"You should have seen it before we started," says Leslie, skipping in a little circle and further confirming my fear that a cheerleading uniform is in her future.

"So, can I help?" Chad asks, but he's not looking at Leslie. He's looking at me.

"Do you mean it?" I ask.

He nods.

It's unreal. It's like my brother actually heard what I said to him yesterday. I told him we wanted him around more, and now he's here, offering to help.

Leslie is saying: "Of course you can help! You're so nice. Come look at the Easy-Bake Oven I found."

It might be too little, too late. I'm not sure if we'll be able to stop Grandma Nora from splitting us apart, but I ask anyway. "Can we use your truck?"

"What for?" Chad asks.

"I want to get this stuff out of here before Mom can stop us."

He nods. "But how are we going to get it past her?"

"I have an idea," I tell them.

Actually, I have two ideas. But I only share the first idea: We'll use the window. It's worked before, so I don't see any reason why it won't work again.

So Chad and I sneak downstairs and do some reconnaissance while Leslie keeps sorting. Mom and Grandma Nora are distracted in the linens room, arguing over a holey pillowcase, so Chad heads out to move the truck alongside the house. He expects me to go back upstairs, but I don't. I sneak into the den. This is my second idea.

The room is much larger and strangely hollow without the cans. I go to Dad's desk and fumble for the power button to the computer. One of Dad's spare deerstalkers is lying on the edge of his desk. I plop the thinking cap on my head. It can't hurt, and it just might help. I close my eyes, trying to decide what to write. It has to be perfect.

The email feels like it takes forever, which is really kind of hilarious, considering the final draft is only three words long.

Dad, come home.

It's scary to ask him to come home. It will hurt so much worse if he knows we need him and he doesn't come. Before, he was ignoring everyone, throwing one of his royal tantrums and hiding behind it. But if Dad doesn't come now, then he's rejecting me. It's personal.

But it's worth the risk. We're on the brink of a Major Catastrophe, and unless I can make Mom and Dad see that we have to change, we're going to be split up for good. I just know it. I can feel it in my bones. They'll end up divorced. Or Grandma Nora will take Leslie, and I'll get stashed with The Real Estate Queen of Tulsa. Chad will go off to college, and we'll never all live together again. We'll lose everything.

I go back upstairs and watch, unnoticed, while Chad and Leslie work together to hoist whole boxes out the window.

They're laughing, and I try to imprint the moment on my mind. It feels precious—the way that something you're about to lose forever is special.

After a minute, I join them and try to live in this moment. I try not to wonder if Dad will get my email. If he'll come. If he'll be able to make it back from England before Mrs. Fix-It puts her latest plan into action.

Box after box.

Bag after bag.

We toss it all out the window. Old stuffed animals and used dolls. Pieces of plastic, choking hazards. Empty shoe boxes. It all rains down on Chad's truck. Scratch that. Most of it rains into Chad's truck. A couple of things hit the edges and bounce out. One particularly memorable box whacks the side of the truck and rubber baby dolls, mostly naked ones, explode across the lawn.

"Whoops," says Leslie, giggling uncontrollably.

"Eh, don't worry about it," Chad says.

"Don't you care that we might dent your truck or something?" I ask.

"It's already pretty beat-up," he says, which is the absolute truth. A few more dings or scratches will be almost impossible to pick out. "Makes me look tough." He grins.

By the time we've tossed out everything that's already been sorted, we've made so much noise that I'm shocked Mom hasn't come to stop us. Even if she didn't see the airborne toys, I don't know how she could have missed Leslie chuckling or Chad shouting "Geronimo!" while he threw ancient Care Bears and headless Barbies into the truck bed.

When we're done, we write a note on the Magna Doodle and run for the truck. We're about to drive off when I pat my back pocket.

"Wait!" I say. "I forgot my phone."

"Seriously?" Chad asks.

"Seriously. You don't even want to know what happened the last time I forgot to check my phone."

Leslie starts to say, "I'm sor—" I don't let her finish.

"Hey," I say, "someone told me that it's stupid to apologize for things that aren't your fault."

Chad gives his head a tiny shake. "If you have to have it, hurry up. I want to get out of here without a fight."

I sprint for the house. He's right. We should hurry. If Mom finds out that we're getting rid of even more stuff without her permission . . . it's not gonna be pretty.

I'm watching my feet so I won't fall on the stairs, which means I don't see Mom until I literally bump into her. She's standing outside Leslie's closed door, reading the Magna Doodle. Her hands are balled into fists. She catches herself on Leslie's doorframe. I bounce off her, landing on my rear end.

"You're taking a load from Leslie's room into town?" she

212

asks. She hasn't opened the door to see what has been taken yet.

I nod. This is it. We're in for a big scene. She'll have a meltdown. Grandma Nora will hear, and Leslie and I will be on a plane for Oklahoma by dinnertime. I just had to have my phone.

She rubs a hand through her colorless hair.

"Yeah," I say. "We'll be back soon." Then I hold my breath, waiting for the fireworks.

But she only nods.

She's not stopping us. She's not telling me no. I can hardly believe it. On a sudden impulse, I grab one of her hands, which is still balled into a fist. "Mom, you have to stop fighting every change we try to make around here." Mom's eyes widen. Whatever she thought I was going to say, whatever she thought I was going to do—this wasn't it.

"I'm trying. But I don't know if I can," she says. The confession is almost a whisper. I grip her hand more tightly.

"Please," I say. "I don't want our family to be split apart. It doesn't have to be this way."

She swallows. I can see the movement in her throat. She opens her mouth and makes a raspy sound, but she can't seem to form a word. Then she pulls her hand from mine. My heart plummets to my stomach.

Then Mom bends down, slowly because of her knees, and picks up a Beanie Baby. It takes her some time to choose one.

Her hand hovers over several of them, before her stubby fingers close around a walrus.

She straightens and holds the stuffed toy out to me.

I take it automatically. I don't understand what's happening.

"What?" I say.

"This one is named Jolly," Mom says. I'm not sure what words she couldn't say seconds ago, but Mom seems to have found her voice again. "I don't think he'll ever be worth much. His tag got torn when your—" She huffs a few times, like she's having trouble catching her breath "—when your father stepped on him one time."

"You want me t-to—take him to town?"

She nods.

"And leave him there?" I feel compelled to clarify.

She nods again.

"Okay," I say. I whirl around and sprint down the stairs before Mom can change her mind or call me back. I'm too slow. I'm at the front door when I hear my name: "Annabelle." I freeze. I knew it was too good to be true. I knew she wouldn't let us leave without throwing some kind of fit. "Annabelle," she says again in a strange, hushed tone. It doesn't sound anything like her usual voice. I half-turn as she says, "Annabelle, I am trying." I wonder if this means she'll fight to keep me. And Leslie.

"Okay," I say.

Her hands are clenched into fists again. "And, Annabelle, no matter what happens, please, please don't hate me."

I close my eyes briefly. When I open them, she hasn't moved. She's standing in the exact same position. I don't think she's even taken a breath.

"I don't hate you," I say.

The Goodwill is in Chatham, but we go right through our own smaller town on the way. We're driving down Main Street when Chad says, "I think Mikey's working this shift. Wanna stop at Exploding Hoagie? He'll hook us up with free drinks."

Chad parks, and as we stroll into the shop, Leslie pelts Chad with questions about his job, particularly the meat slicer, which strikes me as funny. I guess I'm not the only one fascinated by it. Even though I'm still a mess inside from my conversation with Mom, I force myself to laugh.

"Can I try it when you're working sometime?" Leslie asks.

"No, I'm not even allowed to use it yet," Chad says. "You have to be at least eighteen."

"Belles?"

I stop laughing. Only one person has ever called me that. Drew is standing next to one of the window tables. Thomas and a few other guys I recognize from school are with him. My eyes dart to Leslie, who half shrugs and gives me a sympathetic look. I raise my hand and wave. I try to smile like I'm happy to see him and not like I want to die from embarrassment. I haven't spoken to him since the Stair Incident. I tried to text him a few times, but I never hit send. Everything I wrote sounded lame or stupid.

"Who is th—" Chad starts to say, but Leslie grabs him by the elbow and tugs him toward the counter, saying, "I want my drink."

As soon as I wave, Drew crosses the restaurant to come talk to me.

"Hey," he says.

"Hey," I say.

"Hey," he says again. He's smiling ear to ear. He looks so cute, like he couldn't be happier to see me, like I just made his whole day by walking into The Exploding Hoagie. Then I feel that I'm smiling back, smiling so widely my cheeks hurt. Smiling even as I curse myself. I must look awful. The I've-been-cleaning-out-the-garage kind of awful: sloppy ponytail, ratty T-shirt, world's oldest pair of sneakers—ones with a hole in the big toe—paint-stained shorts.

There's an uncomfortable silence.

I can feel Leslie and Chad and Chad's friend Mikey and Drew's friends all watching us. My mind races: What am I supposed to say? It seems like a bad time to go into detail about my family problems or to explain why I was shrieking like a banshee the last time he saw me.

I'm about to blurt out *See you later*, but Drew speaks first.

"I, uh, that is, Rae said that you were going to the cabin with her family this morning."

"You talked to Rae?" I ask, wondering why she never said anything to me about it.

"I just texted her." He shifts a little. "When I didn't hear back from you the other day, I wanted to know if you were okay."

I take that in. "There was a, um, change of plans with the cabin and all."

"Well, is everything—you know—okay?"

I'm about to nod and say, *It's fine*. That's what people are supposed to say, isn't it? But instead the truth pops out. "Well, actually, it's not. My family has some problems. I mean, you saw our house."

He tilts his head to the side, as if he's thinking about this. "It's cool," he says.

"No, it's not," I say. "It's horrible. I didn't want anyone to know."

He huffs a little. "I don't mean cool like 'good.' I mean cool like 'it's all right.' I won't tell anyone if you don't want me to."

"Really?"

"Really."

There's a pause, and I make a quick decision. He's already seen the house anyway. Before I can change my mind, I shake my head and say, "My family's all messed up. *I'm* kind of messed up."

It feels like an earth-shattering confession to me, but he just shrugs.

"Who isn't?"

The words are unexpectedly sweet. They are just what I needed to hear. Without thinking, I throw my arms around him. Over his shoulder, I see his friends elbowing one another and making faces. Thomas is openly pointing.

And if that isn't awkward enough, Chad appears at my side.

"So are you gonna introduce us?" he asks.

I let go of Drew and jump back. Drew's ears are red. Great. He'll break into his Olympic speed-walking routine again any second now. I wish the floor would open up and swallow me whole.

The universe doesn't send a bottomless chasm, but it does send my sister. Leslie walks over and hands me a fountain drink. "I got you Sprite," she says. "Hi, Drew. It's good to see you again."

"Hi," he says.

"Have you met our brother?"

Drew shakes his head, and Leslie introduces Drew to Chad, saying, "This is my friend Dylan's cousin. Dylan and his family are our new neighbors."

Chad gives Drew a nod. Very macho. Then he crosses his arms over his chest. "I'm Annabelle and Leslie's older brother. I'm a senior in high school." He makes the words sound vaguely threatening.

Somehow I survive the next three minutes and get Chad out to the car. Leslie follows us, looking like she's about to pee her pants from trying so hard not to laugh.

"What was that?" I ask Chad once we're out on the sidewalk.

"What?" asks Chad with an evil grin.

"You know what!"

"What do you want me to do when my little sister plasters herself to some guy in the middle of a restaurant?"

"Wow," says Leslie, still dancing with all the laughter she's holding in. "Your face is so red, it's practically purple."

"Shut up. Both of you." I climb into the truck and turn my face toward the passenger window. Mostly so Leslie won't comment on my red cheeks again. We pull away, and I happen to catch a last glimpse of Drew. He's back at the table with his friends. He lifts his hand in a little salute. I smile and wave back. If my family and I haven't scared him off yet, I guess nothing will. It's good to know that real friends will stick with you, even through your crazy.

But the happy feeling starts to fade almost as soon as The Exploding Hoagie is out of sight—because it dawns on me that Drew is just one more thing I'll lose if we can't fix things at home. If Dad doesn't come home. If Mom won't change. If Grandma Nora gets her way. If I end up moving a thousand miles away.

We swing by the high school parking lot and drop our trash bags in the Dumpster. Then we head to the Chatham Goodwill. We pull up behind the store, and a man comes out to help us unload.

"That everything?" he asks when we've stacked the last box on his dolly.

"Wait, what about this?" Leslie has been sitting in the cab, and she sticks her head out the truck window, waving Jolly the Walrus.

"No!" I practically shout.

Chad, Leslie, and the man with the dolly all stare at me.

"I mean, *no*." I try to sound nonchalant.

On the drive home, Chad and Leslie take turns choosing songs on the radio. I hold Jolly on my lap and stroke his silky skin, trying to figure out, after years of fantasizing about turning Mom's Beanie Babies into a bonfire, why I couldn't give away Jolly. Mom gave me permission, her blessing, to get rid of one. It's practically miraculous. And here I am bringing a nonessential item back into our home. Voluntarily. Another miracle. I'm still fiddling with the stuffed toy as Chad turns

221

up our long, unpaved driveway, and our weird day gets a little weirder. Apparently, it's an afternoon for the miraculous. There's a red suitcase on our front porch.

Leslie points and shrieks, "Dad! It's Dad!"

Our moment of reckoning has arrived.

Leslie all but mauls me in her rush to climb over me and out the passenger door. She dashes up the steps, but instead of running through the front door like I'm expecting, she runs down the length of the porch, right past the suitcase, and only then do I see Dad. He's sitting in a chair at the far end of the porch. He stands up and holds his arms open. Leslie throws herself into them.

"Dad, you're back. I'm so glad you came back." She wraps her arms around his neck.

Chad and I walk through the mess much more slowly, less ready to forgive. My hands feel shaky and strange. I'm scared. Sure, he's here. But I have no idea what he's thinking. He might be here to tell us that he and Mom are breaking up.

Or maybe he'll think Leslie and I should go with Grandma Nora. And I don't know if I'll have the words to convince him that our family is worth saving.

Dad sets Leslie on her feet, but she stays glued to his side. She hasn't taken her eyes off his face, like she's afraid he'll disappear if she blinks. Chad and I stop a few feet away.

"Chad, it's good to see you," Dad says.

"Hi, Dad." Chad doesn't move any closer, doesn't reach out to shake Dad's hand or hug him.

"Hello, Annabelle," Dad says. Like Chad, I keep my distance.

"Hey, Dad."

There's an uncomfortable silence. He looks like he wants to hug us, but no one makes a move. Then Dad says, "I got your note."

This surprises me. I was assuming he must have decided to come home long before I hit send on the email. It's, like, a ten-hour flight from London to Colorado, and it's only been a couple of hours since I wrote to him.

"How did you get here so fast?" I ask.

Dad sighs. "I made it as far as the airport, and then . . . I never got on the plane."

"You mean you never left?" I ask.

"No. I've been at Rob's place." Rob is one of Dad's teacher friends. "He agreed to lead the UK tour this summer, so that I could come back and deal with things at home."

"Took you long enough," I say.

"I was hoping your mom might do better without me for a little while, but then I got your email, and I knew I couldn't stay away any longer."

After days of silence from him, I didn't really think my email would work.

But it did. He came home. I asked him, and he came. Maybe I am broken. Maybe all of us are. At this moment, I can't pretend to myself, or to anyone else, that I am whole and unhurt. I feel like I am shattering in a dozen different directions. I look from Dad's hopeful expression to Leslie's huge smile to Chad's crossed arms, and I take a deep breath. I try to ask Dad why he thought things would get better without him. Instead, I do the one thing I've been fighting for days.

I burst into tears.

One minute I'm standing there all normal and mostly calm, and the next—without any kind of warning—I am sobbing: loud, wet, messy sobs.

"Oh, Annabelle. Don't." Dad pulls me into his arms. I feel Leslie's scrawny ones circle me, too, which just makes me cry harder. My shoulders shake, and I can hear the snot dance around with every deep, shuddering breath.

Dad's still holding me as he moves to sit on a wicker bench. He keeps me pressed to his side, and Leslie plants herself on my other side. I don't know how long we stay there.

No one says much. They just sort of quietly cluster around me and hold together the pieces while I fall apart.

Eventually, Chad mutters something about moving the truck. His footsteps fade down the porch. I hear his truck roar to life, and then Chad's footsteps return. There are still tear tracks on my cheeks when he gets back, but I'm calmer now. I look up from Dad's shoulder where I've buried my face and watch my brother lean against the porch rail.

Chad's expression is carved in stone. He didn't seem too happy with Dad before I had my little meltdown, but now my easygoing, carefree brother looks furious. As I quiet, still taking heaving breaths but not actually crying, Chad is the first to speak.

"You shouldn't have left us like that," he says.

Dad pats my back. He doesn't defend himself.

Chad continues: "Do you know what it's been like around here? You haven't called or emailed. I know you're pissed at Mom, but she's been a wreck without you."

I cannot believe that Chad, who's hardly been around before today, is the one saying all this. I start to giggle, but it comes out as part giggle and part sob. I take a deep breath, trying to steady myself.

He's still not done. Chad motions in my direction, waving his hand in an up-and-down gesture. "I mean, look at this. You broke Annabelle. She never acts like this."

I lose the battle with hysteria.

"But I already was broken. I just didn't know it." Those are the words I try to say. They come out in a mush of syllables and sobs and giggles. I'm laughing, but tears are streaming down my face again. So much for my ironclad control of my emotions. The more I've tried to push them away, the worse they are when they fight their way to the surface.

Dad grips me by the shoulders. "Annabelle," he says. "You're starting to scare me. You need to get a grip."

"Should we get her a paper bag?" Chad pulls away from the rail. "Or slap her or something?"

"No!" says Leslie.

"No, no, I'll be fine," I say, and the words are more understandable this time. I bury my face in my hands and block everything out. I stay burrowed there for a few minutes and concentrate on my breathing. I hear voices but ignore them, and when I emerge from my cocoon, everyone is watching me. This time I feel much more in control and ready to talk. I pull away from Dad's side, so I can look him in the eye.

"Why didn't you call us?" I ask.

"I did," he says.

"No, you didn't," Chad says.

"I did," Dad insists, "but Nora convinced me not to call again."

"What? Why?" I ask.

Dad heaves a big sigh. "I haven't even gone back in the house yet," he says. "Your mother doesn't know I'm here. I'll tell her everything I'm about to tell you, but please let me be the one to say it."

"Are you going to fight again?" Leslie asks.

"Probably," Dad says. "I wanted to come sooner, but Nora convinced me that it would better to stay away. She and your aunt Jill feel that I've been 'enabling' your mother. They convinced me that if your mom thought she really was about to lose everything, then she would be forced to change, and I was desperate enough to try it."

"But what about us?" Leslie asks. I'm surprised to hear Leslie say this. She's usually so forgiving, so ready to avoid conflict and make peace. I keep forgetting that she has steel in her, that being soft or sweet doesn't mean being spiritless.

"I thought it would be easier just to stay out of touch with everyone." Dad reaches over me to squeeze Leslie's shoulder. "But I don't know if I made the right choice." He says it gruffly, as if he's making a confession, and it's a confession I don't really want to hear. He sounds as lost as Mom did when she sat out on this porch, on those steps, talking to Grandma Nora. My whole life I thought parents were supposed to have the answers, and now I know that they're just making it up as they go, too.

"It's just . . ." Dad says. "I didn't quite see how bad our home had gotten until that day. Then the newspapers fell and I found Leslie's articles and I knew something had to change, but I didn't know how to change it. I didn't know what to do."

"What articles?" Chad asks.

"I'll tell you later," says Leslie.

A bird caws from one of the aspen trees. There's a longish quiet, and I don't know what anyone else is thinking about, but I'm thinking about Leslie's nightmares and sharing secrets, and what will happen if our family is split up. Everything is messy and uncertain and scary, but whatever happens, I don't want to just watch it all unfold. I want to do something.

I'm the one to break our quiet. "You're right," I tell Dad. "Something has to change. We have to change. You and me and Chad. We have to stop running away. We have to stop keeping everything secret. We have to get help."

"For Mom?" asks Chad.

"Help for all of us."

Dad nods. "I didn't mean to hurt you kids, but the time away did give me some clarity."

His voice is suddenly stronger, and I wonder if Amanda was right about people needing to run away sometimes. It's a bad habit, and it's no way to live. I can say that from experience. But this time, Dad ran away, and he came back different.

Dad stands up and offers me a hand. "Shall we?" he asks with a nod toward the front door. I wipe my cheeks and eyes one last time. Leslie stands. Chad joins her. And I place my hand in Dad's.

He pulls me up from the bench, and the four of us go in search of Mom.

We find Mom and Grandma Nora in the linens room.

"Is that you, kids?" Grandma Nora says without looking up from the pile of old towels she's digging through. "I thought I heard the truck pull up."

"Yeah, it's us," Chad says.

"And me, too," says Dad.

Mom whirls around, scattering a pile of washcloths as she does so, but no one really notices. Then she's in Dad's arms, and there are more tears and sobs and partial questions and hiccups and unfinished exclamations. It's uncomfortably like watching my own breakdown. One by one, starting with Grandma Nora, we slip from the room and leave Mom and Dad to talk.

I head for Leslie's room, but my feet carry me to my own room instead. Grandma Nora is sitting on the floor. Both her suitcases are wide-open in the middle of the room. There is a heap of clothes on the bed, and her toiletry bags are out on the desk.

"What are you doing?" I ask.

"Packing."

"You're leaving?"

She nods.

"Alone?"

Grandma Nora pauses her folding. "What does that mean?"

"Last night you threatened to take me and Leslie away."

She scrunches her forehead. "How could you say that? It wasn't a threat. I only want to help."

"Well, I don't want to move in with Aunt Jill."

She gives a dry laugh. "I got that impression when you ran from the kitchen like your pants were on fire." She places the folded shirt in her suitcase and starts on the next piece of clothing.

"I want to stay here and keep trying to make things better."

She's silent. So I try again.

"You could stay, too," I hear myself offer. "Why are you leaving so fast?" I don't know why I'm asking. I want my room back, but Grandma Nora looks . . . defeated.

She shakes her head and starts smoothing out the clothes already in her suitcase. "I'm clearly not the right person to help your mother, and, well, I convinced your dad to—"

"I know," I say. "Dad told us."

"Oh," says Grandma Nora. "Then I'm surprised you had to ask why I'm leaving. I just figured—after your mom finds out what I did, it's probably best if I go."

I slide down the doorframe and sit sideways across the entrance, putting my feet up on the door. Grandma Nora goes back to her packing. I gnaw on my bottom lip, silently asking a question. Grandma Nora is blissfully unaware that I am trying to say something and the longer I sit there, the harder it is to speak. Finally, I just force the words out. "Why do you think I'm like my mom?"

"Hmm?" She looks up from the pants she's smoothing the wrinkles from.

"On the stairs, when you said that you're broken, you said that I'm like my mom. What did you mean?"

Grandma Nora drops the pants and scoots over to my spot in the doorframe. "I didn't mean to upset you when I said that." I don't answer her, just wait to hear what she'll say. "It's just that you're both so intense."

"Intense?" I ask.

"Yes, you both have such strong opinions, and you both want things to be a certain way."

"Uh, Grandma Nora, have you seen the way my mom keeps our house?"

"Exactly," says Grandma Nora, as if I've just proven her point. "It's a disgusting mess, but there's a system."

I think about it. Alphabetized Beanie Babies. Newspapers ordered by weather report. The toy piles. The brands of canned food. Even the milk jugs and egg cartons were sorted by expiration dates.

"But Mom won't get rid of anything, and I get rid of everything."

Grandma Nora shrugs. "It's the same trait, only expressed in different ways." My head feels like it's spinning. I can see what she's saying; I just don't want to see it. And Grandma Nora's not done. "It's two sides of the same coin. You're both proud. You don't want others to know how you're really feeling. You both try to cover it up until you can't hide it anymore. You love deeply, but have a hard time expressing it. You're independent, too. They're really wonderful traits, but they can be dangerous when neither of you is willing to ask for help or to admit when you've been hurt."

There's a part of me that wants to plug my ears and stamp my feet and scream. But if I did that, I'd probably turn around to find Drew standing in our hallway. And anyway, there's an even bigger part of me that wants Grandma Nora to keep talking to me like this. Like I'm a grown-up. So instead of throwing a tantrum, I ask a question: "Grandma, what do you mean 'when you've been hurt'? What's hurt my mom?"

She doesn't answer right away, and I think Grandma Nora is deciding what to say and how much to say. "Your mother's had a lot of loss in her life, you know. And sometimes the more a person loses, the tighter they hold on to things. Sometimes they start holding on to the wrong things."

"What losses?" I ask. "Grandpa George?"

"Yes. Grandpa George. But he was the second father she lost. Jill was too young to remember their father, but your mother was old enough. She remembers losing her real dad. And then George and then . . ." Grandma Nora trails off, like she doesn't know if she should continue.

"And then what?"

Grandma Nora starts running her finger through the carpet. She doesn't look at me. "We've had some disagreements over the years. It's caused a lot of stress, and she blames that for . . . Did you know your mother was pregnant after Leslie?"

"What?" I ask, sitting up, pulling away from the door-frame. "She was? What happened?"

Grandma Nora licks her lips, still looking at the carpet. She opens her mouth. Shuts it. Opens it again. Finally, I can see her come to a decision. "I'm sorry, Annabelle. It's not my story to tell. You'll have to ask your mom, if you want to know more."

I feel my shoulders slump, but I don't argue with her.

She's right. If I'm going to have this conversation, it should be with my mom. I've never tried to understand her before. I never wanted to.

But it's kind of a funny thing. I'm starting to realize that sometimes, with the people who love you, when you need something, all you have to do is ask. It's not always that simple. Except that sometimes it is.

"When does your plane leave?"

"I thought I'd go standby. There are a few flights out tonight. I'll leave as soon as I'm done packing." She scoots back over to her suitcase and finishes folding the pants.

I lean back on my doorframe and twirl a strand of hair around one finger.

"Can I sit here while you finish packing?"

She nods. "I'd like that."

The room is quiet, punctuated only with Grandma Nora's muttering about where she left this or that. A few times she sends me on errands to various parts of the house. I get the feeling she's avoiding my parents, that now she's the one who's running away. I don't try to stop her. This is something we have to fix from the inside out, and even though Grandma Nora is family, this isn't her house.

By the time Grandma Nora is done, my room is as spotless as when she arrived. She summons Chad to carry her bags downstairs when her taxi pulls up. Before climbing in the yellow car, she hugs me goodbye and whispers in my ear: "Whether you want it or not, I need you to know there's always a bed for you or Leslie at my house." This time it doesn't sound like a threat. It's comforting.

After she's gone, I go back to my room. It feels strangely hollow without her.

It takes me a while to track them down—one is still in Chad's truck, and the other is in Leslie's room—but eventually I find Jolly and Miss Ears. I place them on my freshly made bed. My room looks a little less empty. It looks good.

I'm lying on my bed with Miss Ears and Jolly, staring at the ceiling and trying to figure out what has happened in the last week or so. We're so far out of our usual routine that I'm not exactly sure what to think. We've had Big Family Kerfuffles before and ended up just as crazy afterward. But this time the family holding pattern is as smashed as my Five-Mile Radius. The way things were has gone out the window, and now we're all just waiting to see where the dust will land, what new pattern will form.

It feels like Mom and Dad have been locked in the den forever.

When I last saw Chad, he was out in the garage. Leslie was in her room, poring over the directions to her Easy-Bake

Oven. There were a lot of cautions about operating safety, and they were starting to stress me out, so I came in here, where I could wait without worrying that Leslie will end up burning down our house while trying to make a pan of lightbulb brownies. Although if she does burn down the house, we won't have to deal with Mom's collections anymore. Problem solved.

I turn onto my side, and my eyes land on the little framed picture on my wall. It's been there so long that I don't usually see it, but today I do. I study it: the field of tulips, yellow and gold and red. Mom said she copied it from a photo taken in Holland. I'm probably biased, but I think it's really good, and it's been there all along.

My phone buzzes. It's Drew. He's inviting me and Leslie to a movie tomorrow night with him and Dylan and some of their other cousins. Dylan's mom has offered to drive us into town. I consider it. Since they live just down the road, Leslie and I can walk over to their place and leave from there. I might be ready to meet our neighbors, but I'm not quite ready to let them meet our house.

Then I notice Amanda has also texted me. She wants to know if we can hang out one day next week. I write back: "Chad's working at The Exploding Hoagie. Wanna get together there on Monday?" Next I send little messages to the other girls, even Rae. Just quick hellos with smiley faces.

Finally, I call for Leslie. I shout for her without bothering to get up from the bed. She appears in my room a minute later. "Wanna go to a movie with me and Dylan and Drew and some other people tomorrow night?"

"Sure," she says. "But have you asked Chad's permission?"

"Oh, shut up."

I let Drew know that we're in, and Leslie curls up next to me on my bed. I tell her she can sleep in here tonight if she wants, but she says with Dad and me home and her room mostly clean, she's not sure she'll need to. We're still lying like that when Dad appears. He smells faintly of pipe smoke and the deerstalker is on his head, but the earflaps aren't tied down. I'll take it as a good sign. Also, he's smiling.

"Family Meeting in the living room. Five minutes," he says. "Now, where's Chad?"

"The garage," Leslie says.

"Okey-dokey." And Dad strolls down the hall, whistling.

"Smoking is bad for you!" I yell after him. He just whistles more loudly.

Five or ten minutes later, we're all seated in a loose circle. Mom and Dad and a bunch of towels are on the couch. Chad is on a kitchen chair. Leslie and I sit in piles of sheets. Dad starts the meeting by announcing that Mom has something she wants to tell us. Mom doesn't say anything at first, and we wait in silence while she plays with the frayed edge of a couch towel. She won't make eye contact, and I start to worry.

I was feeling more than half-hopeful when we came down, but now I'm uncertain again. Partly because Mom is not wearing a muumuu.

For the first time in weeks, months, maybe years—I'm really not sure how long it's been—she's wearing a pair of faded black pants and a baggy gray T-shirt, and now I'm not sure how to read her mood. The clothes seem like they should be a good sign, but Mom looks so serious that I don't know what's about to happen.

Dad takes her hand and squeezes it. Mom looks up at him, and she gives him a teeny smile. He doesn't let go. Still clutching his hand, Mom faces us. She licks her lips, presses them together tightly. Then she speaks.

"I'm a hoarder."

Understatement of the century. This is like calling a Family Meeting to announce: "The universe is big" or "Dad likes Sherlock Holmes." I'm mildly annoyed . . . until I realize that I've never heard her use that word. By some unspoken agreement, no one in our family uses that word. Ever.

There's another uncomfortable silence.

Then Chad winks. "We kinda noticed, Mom."

As usual, he says it in a way I couldn't. He says it in the perfect way. He breaks all the tension in the room, and even Mom chuckles.

"That was hard. I don't know why that was so hard to say." Mom twists the frayed towel threads with her free hand.

"It's because we don't like to admit when we have a problem," I say. I don't mean to say it out loud, but the confession just sort of pops out.

Everyone looks at me.

"It's something Grandma Nora told me," I say. I gather my courage and look straight at my mom. "It's one of the ways we're alike."

Mom gives another shaky laugh, but she still looks a little worried. Dad takes over.

"Your mother and I have talked, and we've agreed that Annabelle is right. It's time to get professional help."

"Like a counselor?" Leslie asks.

Dad nods. "We need advice from someone we're not related to. I believe your grandma Nora and even Aunt Jill truly want to help, but sometimes it's easier to accept help from someone outside the family. Someone who won't be as . . . emotionally involved."

I think of Leslie and her nightmares and her anxiety. I think of the way I've been boxing up all my worries and ignoring them. I think of the way Chad has hidden from all our problems at home with parties and buddies and a dozen different girlfriends, and I say: "We should all go."

Dad nods again. "You think we should see a family counselor?"

"Yeah," I say, feeling a sense of rightness. This is something we all need to be part of.

"I do want things to change," Mom says. "It's just really, really hard." She drops Dad's hand and gets to her feet. "Come on, there's something I want to show you all." She walks from the room, and the rest of us sit there for a moment. Even Dad looks puzzled. I guess this next part of the meeting wasn't on his agenda.

Leslie is the first to follow Mom. Dad's next. Then Chad and I glance at each other. He raises his eyebrows, and I shrug. We stand at the same time. When we catch up to the others, Mom is pulling the family portrait in the downstairs hallway off the wall. It was taken just before Grandpa George died, just before things started piling up. It's been hanging there for years. The wall is a slightly different color behind the portrait.

"What are you—" Dad starts to ask, but he cuts himself off as Mom pulls a key from the back of the frame.

She removes the tape and walks over to the Forbidden Room. That's when I understand what's happening. I think of all the fights they've had over these doors, of all the times Dad threatened to knock them down or to call a locksmith, of all the times Mom fought back and begged him to leave it alone. I think of all the endless guesses I've made, trying to figure out what she's keeping in there.

And now she's going to open the ex–dining room. That's when I finally believe Mom is serious. She's not just telling Dad what he wants to hear. She's not just going through the motions. She really does want to be different.

I should have known when she handed me Jolly.

But the trust between us has been so broken for so long that believing her is a habit I will have to relearn.

The key sticks and doesn't want to turn. Mom fiddles with the knob, and I run through my litany of guesses about what we'll find on the other side—cat skeletons, used tea bags and coffee grounds, cash from a lottery she won but never told us about—I feel like nothing could possibly surprise me.

The door to the Forbidden Room clicks open.

And I am astonished.

Because when I see inside, it's our dining room. Not an ex–dining room. Not a Forbidden Room. It's just our dining room, and it's immaculate. It's neater than it was before Mom started hoarding. Our house, even before Grandpa George's funeral, was always messy. Cleanliness was never one of Mom's issues. But the dining room is perfect. No mess anywhere. No papers scattered on the table, no toys on the floor, no wadded-up, used napkins waiting to be discarded. It's musty in the room, and it could definitely use a good dusting, but still . . .

"Wh-where's all the stuff?" Chad is the first to find his tongue.

Mom shakes her head. "This is it."

"I thought it would be full of old tires," says Chad.

"Or decorative pillows," Dad says.

"Or rocks," says Leslie.

They look at me.

"Anything. Everything. Just not this."

Mom is holding her hands together so tightly that her knuckles are turning white. "When I saw that the house was getting to be . . . more than I could handle and I couldn't stop myself from making it worse, I closed up this room. I wanted to save something. I know it doesn't make sense, but it felt like, like everything would be okay if there was just one thing I couldn't ruin."

"You know, Mom," I say, "most things can be fixed even after they're broken."

Dad pats me on the shoulder once in reply as he passes by. He is the first to enter the room. He crosses the threshold, strolls over to the china cabinet, and starts pulling out the wineglasses we haven't seen in years.

"What are you doing?" Mom follows him into the dining room.

"Celebrating," says Dad. "Chad, go to the kitchen and find something we can toast with. And grab a dishcloth, too," he adds, blowing a tiny dust bunny from one of the glasses.

Chad returns a minute later with a dish towel and a two-liter. "It's warm," he says.

"That's all right," Dad tells him.

Leslie follows Chad into the dining room, and she starts wiping out the wineglasses while Chad opens the ginger ale. I stand in the doorway and watch the scene play out.

Our problems aren't over. Our family is still broken in a lot of ways. Mom's not perfect, and a counselor isn't going to make her that way. But Leslie's optimism must be rubbing off. Because for the first time in a long time, I believe that our broken pieces will hold together. We're going to be okay. We're going to be better than we were.

"Come on, Annabelle." Leslie is holding out a streaky, half-full wineglass.

I take it from her and join them in the dining room. I can see specks of dust floating on the golden surface of my ginger ale. They're being pushed around by the popping bubbles. But I don't complain. I'll clink my glass against theirs and pretend to sip my grimy ginger ale.

Dad makes a toast, but I don't really listen. Instead, I look from face to face, and I'm filled with the kind of warmth that soothes over and fills in the cracks. When I look at Mom, it strikes me for the first time that our eyes are the exact same color, the exact same shade. And I make another decision.

One day soon, I'll ask my mom to tell me her story.

ACKNOWLEDGMENTS

I would like to thank my fabulous agent, Linda Camacho.

Without her initiative and enthusiasm, this novel would still be languishing in a file on my computer.

I owe an enormous debt of gratitude to Scholastic, especially to my editor, Emily Seife, for her guidance and encouragement.

I am grateful to the community of writers I encountered through Vermont College of Fine Arts. I particularly wish to thank my classmates, the Allies in Wonderland, for their support and friendship.

I am also grateful to my VCFA advisors: Tom Birdseye who helped me find the humor in my writing; Shelley Tanaka who encouraged me to write a story about sisters; Martine Leavitt who steered me in the right direction; and Sarah Ellis who taught me how to revise.

I am indebted to my critique group, the Charglings, for all of their insight and feedback, and to the staff and students of James Madison Preparatory School who have graciously accommodated my love of both teaching and writing. Lastly, to my amazing friends and family, especially my parents— thank you.

ABOUT THE AUTHOR

Mary E. Lambert is a middle school English teacher at a charter school in Tempe, Arizona. In 2014, she graduated from the Vermont College of Fine Arts with an MFA in children's writing. This is her first novel. Find her at maryelambert.com or on Twitter at @MaryUncontrary.